and Their Adventures with Kitty the Cat

Also by Mickey Hadick:

Ten Stories

Fugue, The Amnesia Love Story That Will Make You Forget
Every Other Amnesia Love Story

Sally and Billy in Babyland

and Their Adventures With Kitty the Cat

Mickey Hadick

Mannon:
I hope you enjoy
this story, and best of
luck in the arts!

PARKSIDE bks

HOLT, MICHIGAN

Best wishes,
Mick Hadick

Copyright © 2017 Mickey Hadick All Rights Reserved.

No part of this document may be reproduced or transmitted in any form or by any means without prior permission of Mickey Hadick.

Disclaimer This book is a work of fiction. Moreover, it is a satirical fable. All characters and events are the product of the author's imagination. Any resemblance to characters, living or dead, is coincidental. That goes double for the talking animals.

First date of publication: September 2017 First Printing: September 2017

ISBN: 9781976295126

Library of Congress Control Number: 2017914355

Book design by Mickey Hadick

Cover design by Michael Reibsome

Artwork illustrations by Michael Reibsome, used with permission

Published by Parkside Books

www.ParksideBooks.net

Blessed are the meek.

Which is nice, because they have a hell of a time.

Sally and Billy in Babyland

and Their Adventures With Kitty the Cat

Mickey Hadick

Chapter One

Sally and Billy thought they were from a happy family but they had no good examples of happy families to compare themselves with and so they got along as best they could. Sally was the eldest and had entered an age of sullen detachment, modeled after many of the girls she admired at school. Billy was full of hope and enthusiasm, conditions that Sally knew Billy would abandon as soon as he came to understand the world.

Their parents tried very hard to make a happy family. On paper, things were fine. Each parent had a good job in the city at an office building with a coffee shop in the lobby. They lived in a house too big for them in a nice neighborhood with wide, smooth sidewalks and rules about cleaning up after your dog. Their father took his turns patrolling for the neighborhood watch, and their mother hosted the candle and jewelry parties every third month, as expected.

And they did things together as a family whenever possible, which wasn't often because of the preponderance of sports teams that Father took Billy to, and the dance, cheer leading, and horse riding lessons that Mother took Sally to.

But this day they would be together and would meet for a picnic.

As was often the case for the family, it wasn't enough to just go on a picnic. They couldn't just go to the local park with neighbors and eat on the grass. It had to be more of an event, and they were meeting at a special, and exclusive, place for picnics.

Their schedules on that Saturday morning meant Sally would be with her mother in the Lexus. It was a nice-enough car but Mother didn't allow Sally to eat inside of it and there wasn't a television to watch.

Sally would rather have made such a long drive in her father's Land Rover. There were video screens on the seat backs and father always kept snacks and drinks inside the built-in cooler.

Billy was riding in the Land Rover, as it so often worked out. During a ride this long Billy would have watched two movies, whereas Sally sighed with boredom 137 times.

At last they arrived, one car following the other like pachyderms, and turned off of the highway at a place with no stores or restaurants, which seemed odd to Sally.

They followed a bumpy road into a vast wilderness area with hills, lakes, and dark forests.

"Where are we?" Sally asked.

Mother smiled back at her from the front seat, glowing with pride. "This is where we'll picnic. Isn't it wonderful?"

Sally scoffed. "If it's so wonderful, why isn't anyone else picnicking?"

"Not everyone has the opportunities you do to enjoy the world." She glanced back at Sally but this time with raised eyebrows in warning.

The bumpy road turned into a gravel road, and then the gravel gave way to tall grass. Mother honked and honked her horn until Father slowed to a stop. Then Mother got out of her car and approached Father's SUV. And not slowly, like a cop, but almost running as she fumed in anger.

"Where the hell do you think you're going?" she asked.

"The impressive stuff is up ahead," he said.

"My car can't drive off-road." Mother motioned toward Father's SUV with a limp wave. "It's not a Range Rover."

"Mine is a Land Rover," Father said. "I don't like Range Rovers."

"I don't care what kind of fucking rover it is. I can't drive any farther."

"Relax," he said. "Why didn't you call me?"

"There's no service out here."

Once they were together in Father's Land Rover, Billy whispered to Sally, "Why's Mom so mad?"

Sally was surprised Billy had even noticed, as he always seemed busy with the games on his phone. "You'll understand when you're older."

"Do you understand?"

Sally shook her head. Why and when her mother became that angry was still a mystery.

Father winked in the mirror at Billy. "What do you think of this, Champ?"

Billy looked away from the television screen. "What are we going to do?"

"Hike in the woods."

Billy considered this for a moment.

"It's something you can tell your friends about tomorrow," Father said, his voice resonating in the cabin of the SUV.

They drove to the edge of the forest and parked.

"Can we eat?" Billy asked. "I'm hungry."

"No," Mother said. "We're hiking first. And besides, I'm intermittent fasting and it's not time for me to eat, yet."

"Well I'm not intermittent fasting," Sally said.

"Maybe you should be," Mother replied quickly.

# # #

With water bottles and granola bars in their backpacks, they set off. Sally and Billy wore hiking boots on their feet, sun blocking insect repellent on their skin, and wide-brimmed hats on their heads.

At first it was fun and exciting to walk through the woods. Sally was the first to realize that 'hiking' meant walking for a long time over rough ground through prickly trees and scratchy shrubs.

Billy stayed close to Mother and Father in spite of his being easily distracted by rocks and sticks, but Sally soon lagged behind. Then she used thirst as an excuse to stop walking.

"Keep up," father urged. "We won't conquer the world standing in one place."

The hike wore on.

Sally and Billy trudged along in silence through the forest, following Mother and Father at a safe distance. The trail was overgrown and there were no markers, but everyone seemed confident that Father would know where they were going. Father seemed most confident of all, and led the way through the trees, pausing only to admire outcroppings of rocks or fallen trees.

Up ahead, Father and Mother were having a heated conversation but Sally couldn't hear what they said. That was not a problem to Sally. Father and Mother had always spoken in heated conversations. Heated conversation was how they spoke about everything.

Usually, Mother exclaimed about an urgent deadline, and Father responded in an agitated tone about a conflicting deadline. Mother, now equally agitated, explained why her urgency was greater, and that Father must pay more attention in the future.

Sally had seen her friends' parents decide things in the same way, but some of those fathers used their loudest voice to get their way, just as some of the mothers used cutting insults. But almost all of them started with heated conversations.

None of it looked like fun to Sally.

Father frequently stormed off in anger, and Mother almost always was brought to the brink of tears that could only be halted with a large glass of wine.

Sally caught up to them at the next fallen tree and overheard more about what was at issue.

"I've had this planned for months," Mother said. "I have to have adult conversation. It's my one night without the kids."

"But it's my poker night," Father said as he kicked at a mushroom growing on the tree trunk rotting into the ground.

"You didn't put it in the calendar."

"Because I play poker every month."

"And I only do this twice a year. So I'm sorry."

"Well I'm sorry too."

Sally knew neither one was sorry. What they meant was, 'too bad.'

They continued on in silence. Sally was not in any hurry to stay near because now Mother and Father would both be in a bad mood.

Billy lagged behind, beating tree trunks with sticks, and moving on once the stick had broken. She envied his ability to stay busy even when their parents were angry about things. Sally enjoyed nothing at such times. If they were home, she would sit in her room alone until the storm had passed.

In a meadow on the other side of a hill, Sally caught up to them and it was clear they were close to a decision. Father was at one side of the meadow with his back to Mother, who sat on a rock on the other side of the meadow as she stared at the ground. Back home, they would lock themselves in their bedroom and argue loudly before Mother came out to announce the decision over a glass of wine. But here the decision would have to be made in some other way, perhaps in a cave or a dense thicket of woods, because Mother thought it set a bad example to argue in front of Sally and Billy.

"I'm hungry," Billy said as he emerged from the forest with an armful of pine cones. Sally watched as Billy threw the pine cones at a squirrel on a branch. She expected one of their parents to yell at Billy, but it was as if they had forgotten about her and Billy.

"I'm hungry too," Sally said, hoping to be noticed.

Billy picked up a branch and beat on the tree trunk. "When can we eat?"

Sally sat down and sighed. "Let's go to a restaurant already."

Mother stood up. "All right, let's head back."

"What?" Father said. "No. We're not even to the trail head."

"You mean we haven't even started?" Mother said.

"No. That's why this trip makes such a great story."

"Family of four dies of starvation?"

"Who?" Billy said. "Us?"

"No," Father said. "We won't starve."

"Then let's go eat," Sally said.

"Okay," Mother said. "We're heading back."

Billy broke his stick across the tree trunk. "But we haven't even started."

Father took on an air of legitimacy. "That's right. The best part is up ahead."

"I want to stay here," Sally said. "We were supposed to picnic."

"I'm sorry but we're still hiking," Father said. He waved for Billy to join him and they walked out of the meadow and back into the forest.

Mother stared after them, her face confounded in disbelief. "Can you believe it?" she said.

Sally lay back on the grass with a sigh. She could believe anything, as she was still just a child, but she knew better than to say such a thing to her mother in an agitated state. Best just to be quiet and wait.

"Well let's go," Mother said. "You and I may as well head back. I can get a sitter, I suppose."

Sally closed her eyes, feigning sleep.

Mother walked beside Sally and bent over her. "Sweetie, let's head back."

"I'm tired."

"You can sleep in the car."

"I want to sleep here."

"I'm sorry but you can't."

Sally did, in fact, want to stay. She had liked the idea of all of them doing something together and still hoped it might happen. A picnic with her family in a grassy meadow in the forest on a day full of sunshine seemed like the best idea. Why her mother hadn't thought to bring along the food was a mystery, but it was because her mother was more worried about getting back for her ladies night than the picnic, just as her father was more interested in hiking the trail than being with family.

She might yet wait out her mother, forcing her to retrieve the food, and then coaxing her father to join them if only for a brief picnic.

"Come on. Let's go."

"I don't wanna'."

"You have to."

Sally rolled on her side away from her mother. She kept her top eye closed, but peeked out with the lower eye. In the grass next to her face, she saw ants and aphids marching up and down the stalks. At the other side of the meadow, a bird alighted on a bush and whistled a tune.

"Oh my God," her mother said as she stepped across Sally's body. "Wait here." Sally watched as Mother continued across the meadow and ventured into the forest where Father and Billy had gone in.

Once she was alone in the meadow, Sally sat back up and looked around. There were other birds in the trees and bushes, and now she could make out their various songs. If she knew how to whistle she might try to imitate them. She made a note to herself to learn how to whistle, but also added a reminder to not share that interest with her friends who might make fun of her for trying.

She noticed other sounds in the forest, and for a moment worried that something dangerous might be lurking about. She decided that if she didn't bother any bears or lions that might be in the forest, they probably wouldn't bother her. And once Mother and Father returned with Billy, she'd have nothing to worry about.

Mother hurried back. At a glance, Sally could tell her mother was not happy, but there was no need to ask because Mother would tell Sally all about it.

"Your father doesn't want to leave, either," Mother said. "He'll get the lunch and picnic here with you and Billy."

"What about you?"

"I have to head back. Your father didn't tell me how long this hike would take, and I am meeting friends. I wish I could stay."

Sally lay back in the grass and crossed her arms.

"I know you're disappointed, sweetheart, but we're all just so busy. You'll understand when you're older and have children of your own."

Sally stared at a cloud and tried to figure out what shape it most resembled. But it wasn't anything. It was just a cloud. So she closed her eyes.

"I won't see you until tomorrow," her mother said. "But I love you."

"I love you too."

Sally heard her mother walk through the grass and into the forest. When Sally opened her eyes, Mother was gone.

Sally kept staring at the clouds. Now she had a little more success with picking out shapes, and saw a kangaroo, and a moose, and a house. Then there was a shape that seemed familiar but she couldn't quite name it. She decided it was a baby. A little, hungry baby.

That reminded her of how hungry she was and she sat up hoping it was time to eat.

Instead, Billy wandered into the meadow.

"Where's Mom?" he asked.

"She left."

"Is she going to get the picnic?"

"No," Sally said. "Dad is."

"No he's not. Dad left to play poker. He said Mom was getting the picnic."

Chapter Two

Sally looked into the forest hoping to see either Mother or Father so she didn't have to worry that she and Billy had been abandoned.

Billy picked up a rock but then dropped it again. "Do you think they left us?"

"No," Sally said. "I bet they bumped into each other on the way to the cars. One of them is probably on their way back with the food right now."

"But the cars were parked in different places," Billy said. "Would they still bump into each other?"

Sally hadn't thought of that. In fact, if they didn't bump into each other in the forest, they wouldn't bump into each other at the car. They might even drive off without noticing that the other car was gone. But she decided to not say this.

"What should we do?"

"I'm not sure."

"I think we should go after them. I bet we can catch them before they leave."

Sally looked around the meadow, unsure of which way she had come in. "Do you know how to get back to the cars?"

Billy shook his head.

Sally looked up at the sun which was now on one side of the meadow. "Do you remember where the sun was when we came into the meadow?"

Billy shook his head.

Sally looked into the forest again, now wishing very

hard that Mother or Father would appear. But it didn't seem to help.

Billy whimpered.

"It'll be okay," Sally said, and put her arm around Billy's shoulder.

"Is it?"

Sally nodded, but she didn't think she could say anything without whimpering herself.

"I don't like being left behind."

Sally nodded again.

They sat down in the grass, and Sally pointed at the clouds. "What does that look like?"

"Mom."

"No it doesn't. It's a house."

"Fine. Whatever."

After a little while, Sally tried something else to cheer up Billy. "Do you remember that time Dad left you at the indoor soccer field because he thought Mom would pick you up?"

"Yeah."

"They figured it out and came and got you."

"Yeah, after everybody left and they turned off the lights."

The shadows cast by the trees seemed a little closer to where they sat in the middle of the meadow.

Billy whimpered again. "Do you think they'll come and get us after the sun goes down?"

"It'll be before that, I'm sure."

But Sally was thinking of Dad's poker nights because she and Billy would 'camp out' on the floor watching movies while Mom sat on the sofa with a bottle of wine until she fell asleep. And on Mom's ladies night out, Dad would order pizza and fall asleep on recliner while Sally and Billy napped on the sofa.

Mickey Hadick

Sally put her arm around Billy again. "They'll be here soon."

# # #

Sally tried to guess how much time had passed by the position of the sun in the sky. But it was much harder than watching the hands of a clock move across its face. She hoped that it meant not a lot of time had passed, and that there was nothing to worry about.

Still, Sally and Billy wore themselves out with hopefulness that turned to terror each time there was a noise in the forest surrounding the meadow. They refused to believe a squirrel or even a tiny bird could raise such a racket among the leaves and twigs on the forest floor, but time and again it turned out to be just that.

And yet, with each fresh snap of a twig, Billy turned to look with renewed hope.

With each sweep of dry leaves, Sally stood up and looked for Mother or Father.

But each time brought the same disappointment.

As the shadows overtook them and a chilling breeze pushed through the trees, a steady noise of steps on the detritus covering the forest floor rose up. The noise brought both Sally and Billy to their feet, as the sound was so much louder than what the squirrels or the song birds had made.

"That has to be Mom or Dad," Sally said.

Billy nodded.

Then the source of the noise was revealed: a family of deer marched in single file into the meadow. A large buck with a growing rack of antlers was in front, followed by a doe. Behind the doe were two fawns, much smaller than the others, and with white spots on their brown fur.

"It's just a bunch of deers," Billy said.

The deer family froze and stared at Billy and Sally across the meadow.

Sally put her arm around Billy and pulled him close, certain that the buck would gouge them with his antlers for trespassing. The look in the buck's eyes reminded her of Mr. Jones in their neighborhood who became irate when Sally once wandered into his back yard.

But the deer ran away, fleeing with their tails up in warning, and springing high into the air across the meadow before ducking into the dark shadows of the forest.

"Whoa," Billy said. "I wish I had one of Dad's guns."

"What would you do with a gun?"

"Shoot those deers."

"That's stupid."

"Isn't that what Dad does?"

"I think he likes to play with guns." But Sally wasn't sure that was right either.

# # #

When the sun had almost set behind the hills in the west, Sally worried about what they should do next. She tried to think of what her mother might do in this situation but that made her angry because Mother had left. That also made her want to cry, but she didn't want to do that.

"Look at that," Billy said. He pointed above the trees where a small, dark object was approaching. It screeched as it shot past them overhead and then landed with a thud against the hill beyond the trees.

Billy stood up. "Do you think it was a bird?"

"No," said Sally. "It wasn't flying. More like falling."

Billy hurried across the meadow.

"Don't," Sally said.

Billy turned and waited, waving at Sally to join him.

MICKEY HADICK

But Sally's feet wouldn't budge. She waved for Billy to come back away from the edge.

"We should go investigate," Billy said.

Sally was against it but before she could say so, Billy pointed at the sky again.

"Here comes another," he said.

Sure enough, another dark object approached from out of the west and screeched as it shot past overhead.

Sally got a better look at it this time, and it was covered in fur, had four legs and a tail.

She tried to speak but her throat closed up and her heart beat quicker. What she thought she saw made no sense. Things were not right. She wanted her mother or her father if only to stand behind them as they sorted this out.

But Sally only had Billy with her. And he looked as frightened as she felt.

Sally took a breath and said in a voice just above a whisper, "I think it was a cat."

Chapter Three

Sally reluctantly joined Billy at the edge of the meadow where they could glimpse the hill through the trees.

"I didn't know cats could fly," Billy said.

"They can't."

"Did they jump?"

Sally thought for a moment. "They must have had help to jump this far."

"We should go take a look."

"I don't think it's a good idea."

But Billy started through the forest toward the hill and Sally followed, worried that whatever they found might be dead. Or that whatever they found might not be dead.

Sally was not okay dealing with the unknown. She was okay with school work, which was just doing what the teacher told her to do. And she was okay with cheer leading, which was doing what everybody else did. And she was okay with riding a horse, which was doing what the horse wanted to do.

But venturing through the woods to confront what might be a very dreadful problem was not okay.

Billy was through the trees first and half-way up the hill when he stopped and just stared.

Sally paused at the bottom to catch her breath. The hill was mostly rock and a bit of grass, an outcropping bathed in the full light of the setting sun, shining through a gap in the trees.

When Sally climbed up to Billy's level, she saw what had

MICKEY HADICK

halted his progress: two kittens, dead, smashed against the stony ground where they landed. One was a Persian and the other Burmese.

"Who would do such a thing?" Billy said, his voice quivering.

Sally knelt down to check on the kitties. They were, without a doubt, dead, like their neighbor's cat that had been struck by a car earlier that summer.

"Look," Billy said. "Another one."

A third dark object approached from out of the sky. Sally moved to catch it, holding up her hands but losing sight of it in the setting sun.

It hit her in the chest and knocked her to the ground.

Sally's chest burned and her head throbbed with pain with every heart beat. She couldn't breathe in or out. Was she dying?

"You did it," Billy said, his voice full of joy. "You saved her."

At last she sucked in a breath through the pain and released a groan.

Billy knelt beside her, cuddling the kitten who had knocked Sally to the ground.

It was not a baby kitten, but an older one, almost a full-grown cat. Its fur was gray with brown mixed in it, and it seemed to have a letter M on its forehead. A Tabby. The kitten blinked as it looked around, and panted. Like Sally, it had had quite a fall.

It stared at the other two kittens lying dead a few feet away, their bodies smashed and broken on the rocky ground. But the kitty did not try to escape Billy's grip or resist his cuddling.

"You're bleeding," Billy said.

SALLY AND BILLY IN BABYLAND AND THEIR ADVENTURES WITH KITTY THE CAT

Sally put a hand to the back of her head and found blood in her hair. She cried, all the fear of the afternoon now pouring out in her tears.

Billy helped her stand up, although not very much because he refused to put the kitten down, and seemed more worried about dropping it than helping her.

"We should go," Sally said.

"But what if there are more flying cats? We have to catch them, too."

Sally looked to the West. It seemed possible that more would arrive. "Wait here and catch the next one. It's your turn."

"Where are you going?"

"I think Mom packed a first aid kit in my back pack."

"Okay," Billy said. "But what about these two?" He motioned with a sad nod of his head at the two dead kittens.

Sally tried to think. "We should bury them. I'll try to find something to dig with."

Back in the meadow, Sally tried to pull herself together. She cleaned the back of her head with a gauze pad from the first aid kit. Mother may have left them in the woods, but at least she thought of that.

As she made her way back to Billy and the kitten, she scrounged through the woods and brought a couple of sturdy branches. "We can use these for digging," she said and offered a stick to Billy.

"You dig. I'm holding onto Kitty."

Sally wasn't in the mood to argue so she found some soft ground nearby and scratched out a grave.

"Let me help," Billy said. "Hold Kitty."

They swapped places. Sally kept watch over the setting sun as she held Kitty in her arms while Billy scratched at the ground with the branches.

Mickey Hadick

"I think it's ready," Billy said. He came and took Kitty from Sally's arms.

"I have to do it?" Sally asked.

Billy nodded and rubbed his nose against Kitty's head.

Sally wished her parents were there. If they were, this was what Mother would tell Father to do.

She scooped up the Persian and her legs trembled. She had never touched a dead thing before, but she made her way to the grave. When she had set it down, she cried. What happened made no sense.

She cried even harder as she scooped up the Burmese. She felt anger well up inside as she laid it down in the grave. Whoever would hurt these kittens deserved to be put in the grave, instead.

Billy helped cover the kittens' bodies and he placed a flat rock as a marker for their grave.

"Should we say something?" Billy asked.

Sally had paid little attention at the funeral when their grandfather died, but things had been said. "I don't know what to say, but I hope these kittens rest in peace."

As they returned to the meadow, darkness settled over them and Sally cried again. Billy handed the kitten to her to cuddle and this helped her stop crying. Then Billy cried and Sally handed the kitten back to him. And so it went with Sally and Billy passing the kitten back and forth until they both stopped crying.

The moon had risen and offered enough light for them to see each other and the kitten, which was between them so they both could pet her at the same time.

"Thank you."

Sally froze. Billy hadn't said thank you, and she herself hadn't said thank you. So who said thank you?

She looked at the pale shapes at the edge of the meadow, but saw no one who might have spoken to them. "Who said that?" she whispered.

"I think it was the kitten," Billy said.

"Yeah," said the kitten. "It was me. Thank you for breaking my fall. And for burying my friends."

Sally stared and Kitty raised its head to stare right back, eyes glowing green in the moonlight. It certainly looked like an ordinary kitten.

"You're welcome," Sally said. "But I'm kind of freaked out, too. I didn't know you were a talking cat."

"Isn't it cool?" Billy said.

"It's not just me," said Kitty. "All cats can talk."

"Then how come cats never talk to people."

Kitty shrugged. "I guess we don't want to be bothered."

"Hey why were you flying?" Billy asked.

Kitty turned her head and flinched. "I'd rather not talk about it. But if you must know, Big Baby is the problem."

"Who is that?"

"No one you want to meet," said Kitty. "Is there any chance we'd be leaving soon? It's not a good idea to wait here very much longer."

Billy smiled. "You mean you want to come home with us?"

"As long as home is away from here, then yes."

"That's great. You can be part of our family."

"I suppose," said Kitty, and purred as Billy rubbed under her chin.

Sally looked around again at the pale shapes surrounding the meadow. "I don't know when we'll be leaving. We're waiting for one of our parents to come back and get us."

"They forgot us," Billy said. "But they'll remember."

"I'm just not sure when," Sally said. "Father doesn't come home after poker night until noon the next day."

Mickey Hadick

"Oh, right."

Sally sighed and glanced up at the moon, taking a deep breath to hold off tears. "And the last time Mother had a ladies night out, they took a bus to Chicago and didn't come home until Tuesday."

Kitty yawned, and a ray of moonlight reflected off of her sharp teeth. "It sounds like you're on your own for at least a day, so we must find a place to hide."

"But why?"

"Because any minute now—"

A dog barked in the distance, and Kitty, tense in their arms, looked in that direction.

"What?" Sally whispered. "What is it?"

"I'll explain later," Kitty said in a sharp whisper. "Follow me."

Kitty jumped out of their arms and sprinted across the meadow and into the dark forest.

Chapter Four

They hid on an outcropping away from the meadow and waited. Her instincts taking over, Kitty situated herself at the edge of the tallest rock with a view overlooking the approach from all sides.

Billy and Sally struggled to find a comfortable perch as they alternated between the desire to see what Kitty could see and relieving the discomfort inflicted by the sharp edges of the rocky outcropping. They scuffed with their feet to climb high enough to peek over the edge, only to slide with a groan back into the crevice.

"You must be much more quiet than that or we're as good as caught," Kitty admonished.

Sally took hold of a mossy edge of rock to stay abreast of Kitty. "But who is it we're avoiding?"

"Border Patrol."

"What border are they patrolling?"

"They call it Babyland."

"Are they babies?" Billy asked.

"No. People that like to be treated like babies."

Sally stifled a laugh. "You're joking, right?"

Kitty shook her head. "It started as a resort for rich people who like pampering."

"Babyland sounds like a stupid name." Billy asked.

"Yes, but they all wear diapers. So it's called Babyland."

Sally groaned. "Come on. I've had geography in school and there was nothing like that on the map."

Kitty heaved a sigh, tiring of the conversation. "The rich

have secret resorts all over the world. The only poor people who know about them are there to do all the work."

"Then why haven't we heard about it on television or websites."

"They wear diapers. So they keep it a secret."

Sally decided it was like the time when she was in the middle-school play and didn't admit to enjoying it because all the other kids said the play was stupid.

"What will happen if we get caught?" Billy asked.

"You saw what happened to those other cats."

"They do that to people, too?"

"Worse. Now be quiet."

Back in the meadow, the moonlight was enough to see. But here on this outcropping, surrounded by tall trees, it was dark. The pale light only penetrated in patches.

They heard the border patrol approach before they saw it. There were many feet tramping through the leaves on the forest floor, snapping twigs. The dog bark they heard earlier was repeated.

A second dog barked in response.

Then a third barked.

And they were all coming closer, the sounds closing in on the outcropping in the dark forest.

"Why didn't we run away?" Billy whispered. Sally could feel the strain and worry in his voice.

"Do you know where to run?" Kitty hissed.

"I guess not."

"Then hiding was our best option. We are down wind so there's a chance the dogs won't pick up our scent. If they do, it doesn't matter where we go."

The shadowy figure of a dog—a Border Collie—moved through the trees and stopped in a patch of moonlight. It made sense to Sally that a border collie would be on the Border Patrol. But it had a tube strapped to its back.

"What is on its back?" Sally whispered, her voice quivering with fear.

"A cannon that fires a net," Kitty whispered. Sally detected a quiver of fear in Kitty, as well. "They trap you with it."

"That's kind of cool," Billy said.

"Not if you're in the net," Kitty replied.

"Shhh," Sally hissed. The sound of footsteps approaching had grown louder, and she was shaking now in fear.

Other shadowy figures of dogs moved through the trees. Sally saw a German Sheppard, a pinscher, a giant schnauzer, and a greyhound. As they passed through moonlight, she saw that each one had a net cannon strapped to their back.

The dogs moved all around their outcropping, sniffing, then looking before continuing the search.

"Anything?" Border Collie asked.

"Nothing here," German Shepard said.

"Zilch," Pinscher added.

Sally was baffled. She looked at Billy and he stared back at her with amazed confusion.

When Sally heard the dogs bark earlier, it hadn't occurred to her they might also have the power of speech. But cats could talk so it was reasonable that dogs could too.

"Okay," Border Collie said. "Back in formation."

"Hang on," Greyhound said.

The wind had shifted and a slight breeze swirled through the trees. The greyhound, visible in the moonlight, looked at their outcropping.

The dogs surrounded the outcropping, scattered through the trees, each one holding its head up to sniff. Sally guessed they were as close as the street was to her front door. Too close to run away.

MICKEY HADICK

One of dogs howled. Then they all howled in a terrifying chorus.

Sally gasped. Billy whimpered. But Kitty snarled and spit in anger.

"No matter what," Kitty said, "stay here and hide. And for the love of Dewey P. Cat, be quiet."

The dogs approached through the trees. As their snouts appeared in the moonlight, Sally could tell they focused on Kitty who now stood up on top of the outcropping with her back arched and her fur puffed out.

"Silence," Border Collie barked. The howling ceased, but one dog smacked his jaws, unable to contain his excitement.

"Come along, cat, and you won't be hurt."

"Go hump a leg," Kitty said. "Unless sniffing your master's butt is more your thing."

Border Collie barked in delight. "Ah, the aloof and indignant feline. How charming. We've all seen what you cats do with your tongues. We've heard your caterwauling in the night. Don't condescend or you'll have no mercy from us."

Kitty crouched down and adjusted her stance on the rock.

"Allow me the honor," German Shepherd said.

"Patience. We have work to do."

Kitty hissed. Then her hind legs twitched and she sprung into the darkness with a blood-curdling roar of "Liberty!"

Chapter Five

A dog yelped in pain, and then another even as the barking thundered—and Kitty snarled—through the darkness.

Then a loud bang, like a firecracker, quieted them all, the explosion echoing through the woods.

The echo faded, all was quiet, and Sally held her breath. Then a scuffling in the leaves was heard and the dogs barked in celebration.

Sally dared to peek over the edge of the rock and saw Kitty ensnared in a net fired from a cannon. She was guarded by three of the dogs snapping their jaws just out of the reach of her claws through the netting.

German Shepherd and Pinscher stood away from the others rubbing their snouts with their paws.

Border Collie inspected and licked their wounds. "Take the feline back to Baby Town. We'll continue the patrol."

"I say we kill her now and eat her," German Shepherd said.

"No," Border Collie snapped. "Bad dog. The feline is not yours. It belongs to Big Baby. See that he gets it."

Once the forest was quiet again, Sally climbed to the top and looked around. They were alone.

"We have to go after Kitty," Billy said. "She saved us."

"We saved her first," Sally said. "We're even now."

"You sound like Dad when he doesn't want to do something."

"Be quiet for a second so I can think."

Billy scoffed. "That's what Dad says."

Sally sat down on the outcropping and looked up at the moon, which was now above them. Nothing else made sense at this point.

"We should go after them and try to help Kitty," Billy said again. "I can still hear them."

It was true. Kitty's angry snarl carried through the forest, followed by a dog's bark. Sally agreed that they could follow, but what would they do if they caught up to them?

"I think we should stay here and wait for Dad. We have to worry about our own problems."

"Now you sound like Mom," Billy said and turned his back to her.

He was right again. Sally hadn't meant to say something Mother would say.

"But what can we do? We're just two little kids. We need to tell adults about this."

Billy shook his head. "That never helps. And they get angry for being bothered."

"Yes, but—"

"Those dogs have Kitty and Big Baby, whoever that is, will throw her through the sky again. Or worse."

"Okay," Sally said, not quite believing her own ears. "Let's follow them."

They climbed down from the outcropping and started through the woods.

"Should we run?" Billy suggested.

"We should try to be quiet. We can't help Kitty if we're caught in a net."

When they weren't sure which way to go, they got quiet for a moment and, sure enough, they heard Kitty snarl and a dog bark. So they followed without getting too close.

As their pursuit through the moonlit forest wore on, Sally grew concerned about her stamina. What had started out as day of hiking had turned into one of abandonment, anxiety, talking cats, talking dogs, and extreme stress and terror. She wanted nothing more than to collapse beneath a fir tree and sleep. This hike in pursuit of Kitty had gone on for longer than their hike that morning. She wasn't sure she could continue.

But Billy showed no signs of slowing down. In fact, Sally had to restrain him so they didn't get too close to the dogs.

They came to a stream in a chasm several feet below where they stood. The reflected moonlight revealed how wide it was—wider than any stream Sally had crossed—and Sally hesitated.

"How do we get across?" Billy asked.

Sally noticed a fallen tree trunk that spanned the stream like a bridge. "They must have crossed there."

Billy approached the tree trunk but waited for Sally. "I think you should go first."

Sally didn't like this at all. All of her activities as a kid were directed by adults. This seemed like a thing they weren't supposed to do. "Are we sure they even crossed?"

"No, but I can't hear them over this stupid burbling brook."

"Maybe we should wait."

"Fine. I'll go."

Billy ventured across, walking and balancing, but then squatted down and sat. "I'll scoot."

"That's a good idea."

Scooting was slower, but felt safer, and the moonlight reflected in the rivulets of the stream sparkled in the darkness.

Sally listened to the burbling murmur of the water slipping past the stones. The sound enveloped her. She felt more relaxed than she had all day, and the scent of pine

MICKEY HADICK

filled her nostrils as a gentle breeze brushed against her cheek.

"Hey wake up," Billy said.

"What?"

"You can't close your eyes. We have to keep going."

Sally snapped out of it, frightened at how close she was to falling asleep on the log.

But when she looked ahead to the other shore, the pinscher dog, its eyes and cannon reflecting the moonlight, stood on the other side.

"I thought so," the dog said.

"Go away," Billy said. "You bad dog."

Sally tugged and pulled Billy back along the log over the stream, away from the pinscher.

But the pinscher stepped out onto the log with a snarl.

"Stay," Sally said.

The pinscher growled, flicked his tail, and the net cannon fired.

Sally blinked and felt Billy bump into her and then she fell into the water.

Sally was shocked and afraid in the water but hit the bottom and stood up, able to get her head out of the water.

As the current pushed her along and she fought for her footing, she looked around for Billy.

But he was nowhere to be seen.

Chapter Six

"Billy!" Sally shouted. There was no response.

She noticed a fallen tree in the water whose branches shook and splashed, and she jumped with the current towards the tree.

Billy was under the surface, caught in the net and tangled in the tree. Sally held her breath and ducked under the water, pulling at the net, and freed him.

As she helped him to shore, she saw the pinscher also entangled in the tree, struggling to keep his snout above water.

Once on shore, Billy coughed up water and gasped.

"Are you okay?"

Billy flopped down on the bank, holding himself up on his elbows. "I think so."

"I'll help the dog."

"What?"

Sally waded back into the stream. She couldn't move the dog because the current had pinned it against the branches of the tree.

Her hands gripped the cannon strapped on its back and she found the buckle and released it. With her help, Pinscher swam away from the tree and onto shore.

Panting, Pinscher said, "I don't know why you helped me, but thank you."

"You needed help. Isn't that what we all should do?"

Pinscher lowered his head but said nothing.

"Can you help us get Kitty back?" Billy asked.

MICKEY HADICK

Pinscher's head snapped back up. "I can't help you with that. The cat belongs to Big Baby."

"Please?"

Pinscher shook his head. "You must leave here. It's not safe for you."

Then he turned and ran up the bank and into the darkness.

Dripping wet and exhausted, Sally and Billy continued on after Kitty. They caught up to the dogs again as the forest gave way to large fields of tall grass. With no trees to conceal them, Sally and Billy slowed down and allowed the gap between them to remain.

At one point the dogs stopped and Billy and Sally dropped to the ground to hide in the tall grass. When they dared peek, the dogs were gone.

They hurried after them, but not running because they were just too tired to run. Sally became confused and anxious as they trotted along in the grass because she recalled when she lost her mother at the mall and she rushed through the crowd after her, convinced that her mother was already in the car driving away while also telling herself that her mother would never leave her behind like that. But here her mother had left her behind, and now Sally was chasing after two dangerous dogs and just as fearful of not finding them as she had been of not finding her mother. And then Billy, trotting ahead of her stopped and waited.

And as Sally came up next to him, her heart pounding and short of breath, she realized what had happened.

The large field of tall grass was on a hill. When they reached the crest, they saw the dogs in the moonlight, below them descending the other side of a hill.

"What is that?" Billy asked.

Before them in the distance was a town, streetlights winking in the dark. Surrounding the town was a dark circle. There was a large building next to a bridge into the town.

The dogs walked past a group of tiny houses, none of them bigger than a shed, and continued on towards the building. They dropped Kitty, still in the net, on the doorstep and barked.

"Okay," Sally said. "Let's go as far as those small houses."

"Jesus, even in the dark I can tell I'd never want to live in something that small."

"Sounds like something Dad would say."

As they approached the small houses, Sally kept an eye on the dogs as a gun-toting guard greeted them near the building.

And when she and Billy huddled up against one of the houses, concealed in the shade cast by the moonlight, they got a better look at the armed guard bathed in the light from the bridge.

"What is he wearing?" Billy asked.

"I think nothing," Sally said. "Except boots and a diaper."

"A diaper? Like he's a..."

"A baby."

The armed guard wearing a diaper raised the gate on the bridge, and the dogs picked up Kitty and trotted across the bridge.

"So now what?" Billy asked. "Sneak across the bridge?"

Sally shook her head. "We have to figure this out. They' ll catch us for sure if we rush into it."

"But they might do something to Kitty."

Sally opened her mouth to speak but instead she gasped as a man stepped around the corner of the building and reached for them. The man grabbed Billy. Sally tried to pull Billy out of the way, but someone grabbed her from behind.

The man covered Billy's mouth with his hand and stole him back around the corner of the house.

Mickey Hadick

Sally kicked and squirmed to get free, but the hands around her held fast and carried her around the house.

She tried to scream but she found she couldn't even open her mouth, and she wished very much that her parents hadn't left them behind in the woods to fend for themselves.

SALLY AND BILLY IN BABYLAND AND THEIR ADVENTURES WITH KITTY THE CAT

Chapter Seven

Once around to the front of the small house, Sally was set back on the ground but the hands holding her gripped even tighter. Billy's captor was a bearded man dressed in a flannel shirt, jeans, and baseball cap with a maple leaf. In the pale moonlight, Billy's face was full of the terror Sally felt inside.

"We ain't gonna' hurt you," the man holding Billy whispered. "We'll let you go but you have to be quiet, understand? It's for your sake. We don't want those guards coming after you."

"Or us," the woman holding Sally said.

Sally nodded and the woman released her. The woman also wore flannel and jeans. Her hair was up in a bun.

"We should go inside," the woman said and opened the door.

Sally hesitated. "That doesn't sound safe either. We're not supposed to go with strangers, even if they have lost their puppy or offer us candy."

"I'm so hungry," Billy said, "I would take the candy."

The woman knelt down. "If you won't come inside, please run away from here. If the guards see you, they'll shoot you. Or worse."

"What's worse than being shot?"

The woman pointed at a dark area on the other side of town. "Time Out."

Her tone made it clear it was bad to be in Time Out but, at Sally's house, Time Out was the place with the biggest television and a pizza oven.

Sally decided that they had been caught and released, so going inside was not dangerous. If the man and woman wearing flannel and jeans wanted to harm them, they would have already.

Once inside, the house felt even smaller than it looked from the outside. The few pieces of furniture crowded each other. There was a small table and two chairs in the kitchenette. There were two cushioned chairs in front of the only window. And there were two doors along the wall.

The man introduced himself as Chuck, and the woman, his wife, as Laurie.

Chuck arranged the chairs so they could talk, and Sally and Billy sat in the cushioned chairs as Laurie made them sandwiches.

"What are you doing outside of the town in the middle of the night?" Laurie asked. "Are you trying to get away?"

"We're trying to get in," Sally said, feeling better just from the smell of food. "We're trying to rescue our cat."

"A pack of dogs caught her in a net," Billy said.

"We followed them here."

Laurie grew somber at this. "The Border Patrol."

Chuck locked the door and peeked out the window.

Sally's fear turned to dread in her stomach.

Laurie lowered her voice and said, "I'm sorry but that town is not a good place for cats."

"That's why we have to rescue Kitty," Billy said with clear conviction.

"Maybe we should talk about it in the morning," Laurie said.

"What does that mean?" Billy said, now worried.

"That's what grownups say when they don't want to deal with difficult things," Sally said. She regretted being mean, but she was too tired to apologize now.

MICKEY HADICK

Laurie folded her hands and leaned closer to Sally. "That town is not a nice place. Those dogs, the Border Patrol, keep people from coming in or leaving. The people in that town hate anyone different, and they can be cruel about it."

Sally thought about this. She turned to Billy and said, "At least we know where Kitty is. Maybe we should sleep a little and figure it out in the morning, okay?"

Laurie took their empty plates. "We should dry your clothes and you children need your rest."

"Okay," Billy said. Then he slumped back in the seat with a yawn.

In the morning, with daylight, the small house seemed smaller still. Sally got up first and used the bathroom, which was almost too small to close the door once you were inside. How these grownups managed baffled her.

Back in the main room, Billy stood on their makeshift bed—the two cushioned chairs pushed together with an ottoman in between—and reached for the ceiling.

"I can almost touch it," he said.

Chuck and Laurie emerged from the other room dressed in the same clothes as the day before. It was then that Sally realized they were poor. These were people Mother referred to as the unfortunates.

"How poor are you?" Billy asked, coming to the same conclusion. "Do you beg for money?"

"No," Chuck said.

"That's not allowed in Babyland," Laurie said.

Sally pulled Billy down on the chair. "Don't be rude," she whispered.

"It's just that they don't seem to have a lot of space or a lot of things. Our playroom in the basement is bigger and has better stuff."

"I'm sure it does," Laurie said. "Most people have more space and better stuff than we do."

"But we have each other," Chuck said, and gave Laurie's hand a squeeze.

They again made them sandwiches—bread covered with a spread from an unlabeled jar.

"We hope you changed your mind about going into Baby Town," Laurie said. "It would be so much better to just run away now."

"But we have to rescue Kitty," Billy said.

"That must be a special cat."

Billy nodded. "It can fly."

"It doesn't fly like a bird," Sally said. "But it did fall from the sky."

"Let me show you about that," Chuck said and pointed at Babyland. "If you look right in front of Big Baby's tower, in the park across the street, you can see a big pole barn. And right next to the pole barn is another thing. Do you see that?"

Sally looked and saw what appeared to be structures for a playground. "I see a contraption on wheels."

"That's a catapult," Chuck said. "They wheel it out of that barn each morning so that everyone can see it."

"What's a catapult?"

"It's a big contraption you use to fling a cat a long way."

"Why would anyone want to do that?" Billy asked.

"For the people in Baby Town, strange and cruel things are normal," Laurie said.

"Why's that?" Sally asked.

"I don't know exactly, but part of it is because of the gas lighting."

"Gas lighting?"

"It's an old-fashioned way of lighting streets, buildings and homes. It makes you think things look one way when, in fact, they look different. So you don't know what's real or fake, or what's right or wrong."

"Why don't they upgrade to LEDs? My dad put them all over the house, and everything seems to be what it is."

"Big Baby prefers that people don't know what's real. Then he always has an excuse."

"An excuse for what?"

"Whatever he needs to explain as being not his fault."

"Oh," Sally said, and thought of the many times she'd wanted an excuse but couldn't think of one. "Billy blames me for a lot of things."

"Yes," Laurie said. "That's the idea."

Billy had grown bored of talking. "What do we do? Get guns and shoot our way into town?"

Chuck shook his head. "They have a lot of guns and lots of bullets. You wouldn't even get onto the bridge."

"Do we sneak in, like ninjas, and creep around until we find Kitty?"

"You would be discovered at some point, and they would throw you out of town. The hard way."

Billy sat down in the chair and crossed his arms. "So what the heck do we do?"

Laurie sat opposite him and leaned close. "Chuck and I discussed it last night. We think we know what will work, but want to make sure you understand that we can't help you once you are in Baby Town."

"You can't come with us?" Sally asked.

"We only go into Baby Town when there's a plugged toilet."

"Ew," Sally said. "Is that your job?"

Chuck shrugged, Laurie lowered her gaze, and Sally realized her mistake.

"Sorry," Sally said. "That was mean. I shouldn't have said that."

SALLY AND BILLY IN BABYLAND AND THEIR ADVENTURES WITH KITTY THE CAT

"We don't like it either," Chuck said. "It's the only work we're allowed to do."

"Why's that?" Billy asked.

"When we first came here, we lived in a nice house, and we worked in a bakery. Laurie worked the cash register, and I baked."

"Then what happened?"

Chuck sighed. "Then Big Baby took over, and he riled up the people with promises of how much better the town could be. He blamed people like us for all the problems, even though there weren't that many problems."

"Big Baby kept telling lies until he found enough people to listen who also wanted to blame someone else for their problems."

"We only came here to help," Laurie said. "But everybody hated us because of Big Baby."

"They fired us from the bakery. Once we didn't have jobs, and ran out of money, they kicked us out of town."

"Just because we are from Canada," Chuck said.

"What's wrong with being from Canada?" Sally asked.

"Nothing. Except Big Baby blamed us for problems."

"So why don't you go somewhere else?"

"We don't have enough money to make it on our own, so we're trapped. Big Baby was going to send us back in chains, like criminals, but then they realized they needed people to do the nasty jobs no one else wants to do."

"Like fixing plugged toilets?"

"Yes," Laurie sighed. "Now I wish they'd sent us back in chains. We're stuck right here, outside of the town, but not anywhere, until we die."

They were all quiet for a moment, each one thinking their own sad thoughts about the situation.

Sally was the first to speak. "After we save Kitty," she said, "maybe we can save you."

MICKEY HADICK

"That'd be nice," Laurie said. "But first we have to get you inside town."

Chuck and Laurie fussed over Sally and Billy, tidying them up as they explained the plan. Then Laurie filled their water bottles and packed the last crusts of bread in the house into their backpacks, and Sally considered not leaving.

But staying here wouldn't save Kitty, and Billy would go after her alone.

Chuck peeked out the window. "No patrols. Just the single guard at the bridge. This seems like the best chance."

"Tell us your story again," Laurie said.

"We are orphans who wish to grow up to be like Big Baby."

"Don't run away from guards with guns," Laurie said. "Anybody running away is considered guilty and shot in the back."

"And what do you hope to do when you grow up?" Chuck asked.

"Be just like Big Baby," Sally said.

"And what else?"

"We hope we can be of service to him until we grow up."

Chuck sighed. "I know it sounds stupid, but it's all we can think of to survive in there."

Laurie nodded and gave them each a hug. "We'll come for you when it's time."

Sally and Billy thanked them, waved goodbye, and walked out the door. They decided their best chance was to not be seen with Canadians—though Sally, for the life of her, couldn't imagine how a guard would know a Canadian on sight—so she walked with her brother toward the bridge into town.

The town looked different in the daylight, just like Chuck had said. The houses on the other side of the trench were

40

larger than Chuck and Laurie's house, but only a little larger. There was trash strewn along the paths and roads, and the trees and shrubs were barren and brown. Then the breeze shifted and a putrid smell overwhelmed Sally, bringing tears to her eyes.

"Do they have to keep people *out* of that mess?" Billy asked. "It's a dump."

Sally tugged on Billy's sleeve and motioned for him to be quiet.

"Holy man, this looks like the part of town where Dad won't stop for red lights."

"Shhh. What if they can hear you?"

"All right stop—"

"Halt," the guard said. He had been around the corner of the building next to the bridge and as he approached there was a rubbing noise with each step. The guard wore a brown diaper, hiking boots, and a canvas cap on his shaved head. Otherwise, he wore nothing else.

From a distance, he seemed like a dangerous soldier. But up close, looking at the nipples on his chest and the sloppy corners hanging out of his diaper, he didn't look so dangerous.

"Are you a soldier?"

The guard sneered, his eyes squinting and his nostrils flared. "State your business."

Flustered, Sally forgot their story.

"We come in peace," Billy shouted.

The guard relaxed and shifted his feet, and Sally realized the rubbing noise came from his diaper which had bunched up between his thighs.

The guard glanced over his shoulder. Sally followed his gaze to the door on the building. There was a sign that read, "Foreigners Not Welcome. Go Back To Where You Came From."

MICKEY HADICK

"What are you kids doing here?" the guard asked. He was sincere, and his eyes looked sad and concerned.

Sally stammered a moment but said, "Oh, we're trying to get into the town."

The guard shook his head. "Just go back. You don't want —"

A strange sound came from the side of the building, a rhythmic rubbing in cadence with marching feet.

It was three more soldiers, each one in boots, a canvas cap on a shaved head, and brown camo-diapers, marching towards them in a hurry, their diapers rubbing between their thighs.

The guard in front of them snapped out of his relaxed posture and put his rifle on his shoulder.

The other soldiers arrived and fanned out around the guard. They pointed their rifles at Sally and Billy.

Then the guard's sneer returned to his face and he joined the others and pointed his rifle at Sally and Billy.

Chapter Eight

There were four soldiers in diapers in front of Sally and Billy. The diapers, fashioned out of brown canvas and attached with large black safety pins at the side, looked ridiculous.

But the rifles pointed at Sally's face made the soldiers seem dangerous.

Sally wanted to turn and run. But she remembered what Chuck and Laurie said about running away so she stayed put.

Sally found it difficult to stand still because her knees wobbled. If only the soldiers would lower their weapons, she might speak.

"State your business," the soldier in front said.

"We seek asylum in Babyland," Sally said, struggling to form the words. "We have run away from home, and wish only to grow up to be just like Big Baby."

The guard nodded. Then he looked at Billy. "What about you?"

"I want to be a soldier, just like you guys."

Sally thought she saw a look of regret on the guard's face.

The other soldiers relaxed and lowered their weapons. Sally breathed at last.

A soldier escorted them to the gate while the guard hurried inside the building.

From the gate, Sally could see down into the trench. At the bottom was water so the trench was a moat. Except that

MICKEY HADICK

there were piles of trash so thick it seemed you could walk from one side to the other without getting your feet wet.

Another soldier came out of the fortified building. This one must have been in charge because he wore a diaper fashioned from tan canvas and he carried a clipboard instead of a gun.

"You have requested asylum?"

"We have," Sally said.

"Come with me."

As the soldier escorted them over the bridge, Billy stumbled over an uneven spot. Sally noticed cracks in the cement and rust covering the girders along the side. It seemed they could let the bridge collapse and then they wouldn't have to guard it so much.

On the town side of the bridge, a foul, rotten stink replaced the smell from the trench. The stench was so thick that all of Sally's skin felt unclean, and she rubbed her arms, neck, and face, trying to wipe the smell off.

The street lamps were on, lit by tiny flames in the glass chambers at the top, and emitting a constant hiss like air escaping from a balloon. Those were the gas lights.

"Call the police," their escort told the guard on duty at the other end of the bridge.

That guard went to the building next to the bridge and spoke into a phone mounted on the wall next to the door.

"Whatta' ya' need the police for?" Billy asked.

Their escort looked at Billy but didn't answer.

The houses nearby were run down. The front yards choked with weeds, toys strewn along the sidewalk, garbage cans tipped over at the curb.

A policeman arrived in a patrol car. He wore boots, a cap, and a diaper fashioned out of dark blue cloth. Because his chest was bare, his badge was attached to the diaper. His gun holster was strapped to his thigh.

SALLY AND BILLY IN BABYLAND AND THEIR ADVENTURES WITH KITTY THE CAT

Their escort conferred with the policeman, who opened the back door of his patrol car. "Get in."

Across the street from the bridge was a large park. A few women strolled along the path while small children played on the grass.

The women wore slippers on their feet, loose smocks—like a baby might wear—and cloth diapers. She wasn't sure, but Sally thought the women's diapers were decorated with rhinestones.

As they drove, the houses surrounding the park gave way to shops. All the shoppers wore diapers.

Then there were small office buildings and several men along this part of the street. All of these men were bald as eggs. Some of their diapers were white cloth. Some diapers were blue or gray, and a few were bold pinstripes. There was even a diaper with an elaborate paisley pattern. Most of these men had large bellies and hairy backs, and Sally wondered if it might be better if they also wore smocks like the women.

"Does everybody wear diapers?" Billy asked.

Sally elbowed him, but he couldn't take it back.

The cop glanced back as he drove. "Here in the nicer parts of town, everybody does. But not everybody can afford diapers. And those people can stay to themselves."

"What about kids?" Billy asked. "Do kids wear diapers?"

"Don't be stupid," the cop said. "Kids don't wear diapers. Just babies and adults."

He stopped the car and twisted around in his seat. "I thought you two wanted to be like Big Baby."

"We do," Sally said.

"Then there won't be any problems."

Sally forced a smile and nodded. When the cop resumed driving, Sally shot a look at Billy.

The cop stopped the car in front of the police station and opened the door for Sally and Billy. "Let's go."

Next to the police station was a tall building, golden and shiny, towering over all the other office buildings.

Billy gaped and gawked at the golden tower. "Whoever lives there must be trying to prove something."

"What's that?" the cop asked.

"Nothing," Sally said, trying to cover. "He means we hope to live there one day."

A limousine pulled up to the curb in front of the big tower and the policeman came to attention and saluted. "Put your hand over your heart."

"Why?" Billy said.

"Because Big Baby is here, and loyal, happy citizens put their hand over their heart to greet Big Baby."

"Is he like a king?"

"Better. We asked him to be our leader."

Sure enough, the people on the street stopped in their tracks and gazed at the limousine while holding a hand over their heart.

Two armed men wearing jet-black diapers got out of the limousine and took up positions around the rear door. Other men in black diapers came out of Baby Tower and formed a line, holding their rifles before them.

When all things seemed in order, the guard at the limousine reached for the rear door.

The security detail snapped to attention, the limousine door opened, and out stepped Big Baby.

Chapter Nine

Sally's eyes widened. First out of the limousine was Big Baby's bald head. The scalp was covered in pink and red splotches and a sad shade of yellow in between. Above his sunken eyes were thick eyebrows, the gray hair twisted like an owl's plume. His swollen face and nose were red and criss-crossed with wrinkles. Jowls flapped at his chin.

Thick arms hung like sausages at his side. A large stomach protruded from his torso and rested like a swollen bottom lip over his diaper. On his feet were golden slippers.

There was a gold medallion around his neck, a gold watch on his wrist, and a gold ring on the pinkie finger of his right hand.

"Is that him?" Billy asked.

"That's him," the policeman said. "That's Big Baby."

Big Baby squinted up and down the street, nodded to those on the street saluting him, and strode past the security detail and into the building emblazoned with his name.

The policeman watched as the security detail returned to the building and the limousine drove away. Even after the street was empty, he looked after where those special forces had been.

"What's next?" Sally asked.

"Huh?" The cop sighed and took one more look back at Big Baby Tower where two of the security guards stood beneath the gilded sign above the door.

"Hey where are the cats?" Billy asked.

The policeman nodded. "Let me tell you about the cats.

MICKEY HADICK

I was on the first detail that cleaned up the cat problem. Went door to door, night after night. I caught or killed as many cats as any man on that security detail. But does that matter..."

Sally exchanged a look with Billy, scolding him with her eyes before he asked another stupid question.

The policeman looked at Sally and scowled. "Get inside."

The cop delivered them into the care of a policewoman who sat them down at her desk. She seemed bothered to fill out the form on their behalf. And when she realized they had no identification papers, she dropped her pen on the desk and sat back, pressing her lips together in anger.

"What do you expect me to do?"

Sally's throat tightened. "We want to live here and grow up near Big Baby. In Babyland. Can you help us?"

"I don't know," the woman said. "Can I?"

She wiped her nose on her blue smock and stared at them. Sally thought of the women her mother dealt with in shops or offices, plain women who looked old at a young age and didn't bother to do anything about it. But, as her mother explained, their anger about their looks was taken out on the world. The only thing to do with such women was to keep trying.

"Would you?" Sally asked. "Please?"

"Aren't you supposed to help us?" Billy asked.

"Don't tell me how to do my job."

Sally lowered her gaze but tapped Billy on the leg, hoping he would shut up.

The woman took up the pen and leaned over the form on her desk. "What is it you want?"

"We ran away from home and we want to live in Babyland."

The policewoman's lips puckered. "Would you care to donate any money to Big Baby?"

"No," Sally said.

"Nothing?"

"We have no money."

The policewoman nodded. One of her eyebrows raised. "That's unfortunate."

Chapter Ten

The policewoman handed them off to a Juvenile Detention officer, who handed them off to the Liaison from the Superintendent of Schools, who handed them off to the Student Counselor at the Big Baby School for the Prematurely Disillusioned.

The school was in an abandoned factory. There were no classrooms; just one large, dusty space with broken machinery scattered across the cement floor. It smelled like gasoline.

"This is where you'll spend your days," the counselor said. "Learning."

Groups of children lackadaisically cleaned, pushing brooms and picking up debris from the floor.

"It looks like they're just working," Sally said.

"That's how you learn."

The counselor handed Billy a broom and shoved him toward a group of smaller children in the middle of the space.

"When is lunch?" Billy asked. "I'm starving."

"We don't serve lunch," the counselor said. "You eat what you brought with you."

"But I have no food."

"Then I guess you'll go hungry."

Sally, who still had the artisanal granola bar her mother stowed in her backpack, gave it to Billy who offered to split it with her. Sally refused. She knew from the various diets her mother had imposed on her that she could go at least another day without eating.

SALLY AND BILLY IN BABYLAND AND THEIR ADVENTURES WITH KITTY THE CAT

Sally was sent into a dark corner where children carried bricks across the factory.

"Watch the oil," the counselor said, pointing at a large puddle in her path. "It might be toxic."

In what amounted to her classroom, there were seven boys and girls carrying the bricks, one at a time, from the pile in one corner to the pile in the other corner.

A man wearing nothing but a diaper sat in padded recliner with torn upholstery, absently watching the children work.

"I guess I'm in this class," Sally said. Up close, she noticed a stain on his diaper that she hoped was dirt.

The man shrugged. "Grab a brick and start learning."

Sally watched a boy around her age pick up a brick and shuffle toward the other pile. She picked up one of her own and followed him.

At the other pile, in the far corner of the building, he dropped it onto another pile of bricks. Sally did the same.

"Welcome to school," the boy said. "I'm Tommy."

"I'm Sally. And is this all we do?"

"Nope," Tommy said, beginning the journey back to the other pile. "One day a week we watch television."

"No talking during class," the teacher said.

They each grabbed another brick and headed back.

After they dropped the brick on the other pile, Sally said, "Wouldn't it be faster if we took two bricks at a time?"

"Doesn't matter," Tommy said. "Once we move them over here, we bring them back again."

"You're kidding."

"No talking," the teacher said. "Unless you want to go to Time Out."

"She needs the bathroom," Tommy said. "Okay if I show her where it is?"

MICKEY HADICK

"Take a brick with you," the teacher said. "Always take a brick."

Tommy led Sally out of the factory to a stand of trees around back. He dropped his brick on the ground and rubbed his shoulders."

Sally also dropped her brick. "This is where you go to the bathroom?"

"Sure."

"Isn't this, like, weird?"

"Does it matter?"

Sally crossed her arms and rolled her eyes. "I suppose you want to show me something else?"

"I do want to show you something else," Tommy said and unzipped his pants. "But first I need to pee." He turned his back and leaned against one tree.

This became yet another incident on a long list of things Sally had seen, heard, or done for the first time in her life during the past day. Still, she was uncomfortable watching Tommy pee.

"Careful," Sally said. "If you shake it more than three times you'll get sent to Time Out."

"The joke is you're playing with it."

"What?"

Tommy zipped up. "If you shake it more than three times you're playing with it. But I wouldn't play with it. The penis has one or two biological purposes, and being a distracting toy isn't one of them. Men say those sort of things because of lingering homophobic malaise."

"Oh. Okay."

"I don't play with toys, anyway. Toys entertain the weak minded and offer temporary relief from the dread of ulti-mate annihilation. But our so-called reality is only an illusion conjured by our brain's interpretation of the senses. Whether we are pleased or disappointed, victorious or defeated, hopeful or despondent — it doesn't matter. It's all a lie we tell ourselves, compelled by evolutionary forces to sustain the illusion."

Sally could think of nothing to say. Her parents had been frustrated or angry at the world, but that was different. It was about money—needing more or wishing someone else had less—not existential questions about the nature of reality.

"Come on," Tommy said. "It's all just an illusion, but I can still show you around."

On the other side of the factory they climbed on top of a large pile of debris and broken equipment for a better view.

"Time Out is over there," Tommy said, pointing at a barren patch of ground with a few huts scattered across the field and surrounded by a barbed wire fence.

"So no one is in Time Out?"

"There are plenty of people in Time Out. They're either confined to the huts, or out on work detail."

"That doesn't sound like the time outs I've gotten."

Tommy shook his head.

A lone figure dressed in a gray diaper marched along the fence. "Who is that?"

"One of the Time Out officers. They make sure you stay in Time Out until it's time for you to leave Time Out."

"It seems awful," Sally said.

Tommy shrugged. "Whether you're in Time Out or out of Time Out, it doesn't matter."

The wind shifted and Sally flinched at the smell. She looked around the pile of debris and noticed a dead skunk. "Can we go?"

"I want to show you something else, anyway."

Tommy led her closer to the corner of the factory and showed her another barren field on the other side of a barbed wire fence.

"And what are those cages?" Sally pointed at a smaller compound on a cement surface with several smaller huts. Each hut was enclosed in its own cage, and the entire compound was enclosed in fence and netting.

"That's the Kit-Kat Klub. Time Out for felines."

"How come no one patrols around that compound?"

"There is no way for those cats to escape. They either die in those huts or they are catapulted to their death."

Sally shuddered and hugged herself. "I'm not sure which is worse."

"Oh, that's not the worst thing that can happen to them," Tommy said. "Every few days, Big Baby comes around and visits the Kit-Kat Klub. He grabs the pussies until he finds one he likes. Then he takes it back to live with him in Big Baby Tower."

Sally thought of Kitty, the kitty she saved, being taken to live with Big Baby, and she bent over and retched, spitting bile on the debris at her feet.

Sally wanted nothing more than to see her mother or her father appear to take her back home. But, even if they did, she wouldn't leave without Kitty.

Chapter Eleven

After school, Tommy invited Sally and Billy to stay with his family since they had nowhere to go.

"Your family won't mind?"

"Even if they do, I'm certain it literally won't matter."

"Literally?"

"Yes, literally," Tommy said. "My father is a devout nihilist. Nothing matters to him."

It turned out that Tommy's sister Wendy was the same age as Billy. The two couples matched rather well as they walked along the street. And the homes looked neater than they had in the morning. It seemed as if a cleaning crew had come by to tidy up the broken toys and trash left in the street.

Sally smiled. "I think it might be nice to live here and raise a family."

"What?" Billy said. "That's not why we're here."

This confused Sally. "I know you're right. I'm not sure why I said that."

"It's the gas lighting," Tommy said. He pointed up at the street lamps. "They don't work over by the school because no one cares what kids think, but here in the neighborhoods they pour it on thick."

Tommy and Wendy lived with their parents, William and Tonya, in a small but tidy house. Sally was glad they she had a place to stay, and gladder still that neither William or Tonya wore diapers.

Sally remembered learning from her mother that, when

55

visiting people, she needed to say something polite and complimentary, regardless of the situation. "You have a lovely home."

"It's a piece of shit," William said. "But thanks anyway."

Sally looked at the family, worried that she may have walked into yet another trap.

"Don't worry about it," Tonya said, coming to Sally's rescue. "We know what's real and what's fake. We like our house, but it is a piece of shit. That's just how we perceive it."

"But what about the gas lighting," Billy asked. "Doesn't that make you think everything is nice?"

"That only works to a certain degree," William said. He assumed a comfortable posture at the kitchen table, which Sally recognized from her father's similar posture at a restaurant.

William scooped food into his mouth and swallowed so he could talk again. "There are other mechanisms that work in concert with the gas lighting to convince people that everything was going according to plan, or that things were as they should be. Foremost is our herding instincts. No matter how bad of a situation it is, as long as other people are suffering, you put up with it."

"That's why they use isolation huts in Time Out," Tonya said. "It makes you crave joining the group again."

"And most people covet what their neighbors have, so they will work to have things just as nice for the social prestige."

"Because no one wants to be shunned for having the worst house in a neighborhood."

"Except for us," William said. "We don't care."

"Because it's all an illusion," Tonya added.

"The strongest influence is our confirmation bias. Once we decide on something, we don't want to admit we were wrong. So you move with your family to a place that seems to be a good place. And once you are there, and you've committed, and you've bought a house, you defend that decision, ignoring the facts about the flaws and the problems, because you don't want to admit you were wrong. That's the confirmation bias twisting your brain."

The family waited to see if he would continue talking. Sally remembered her own father pontificating at the restaurant tables, but he never talked about ideas such as these. Sally's father complained about the food, or the service, or someone at work who had betrayed him that day.

William seemed about to scoop more food into his mouth but lifted his head to speak. "The same things happen with jobs. You see people working at a certain place and, from the outside, it looks like a great place to work. You'll do anything to work there. And, if you do, you ignore the flaws and problems because of bandwagon bias. Instead, you covet someone else's job, and continue to work to get that job, or a measly two-percent raise, or a free donut in the break room."

"If you seem to know so much about bias, fallacies, and the false perceptions of your existence," Billy said, "how come you stay in this piece of shit house?"

"I'm glad you asked," William said.

"This is the boring part," Tommy said, and put his head on the table.

"Be respectful," Tonya said. "Even if all of this is just an illusion, he's still your father."

William rose to the occasion, standing at the head of the table. "Because I only suspected these truths when I brought our family here. I hadn't found the deep understanding needed to navigate our perceptions in a way that mattered. And then something terrible happened. One of our family was taken away from us, grabbed right out of the

MICKEY HADICK

sanctity of our own home, and in spite all of our efforts to rescue her, we failed."

William sat down and resumed eating.

"I'm so sorry," Sally said. "What happened?"

"They took our cat from us," Tommy said. "It was during a *correction*. Men with guns arrived in the night and took her away and we never saw her again."

"Why didn't you fight them?" Billy asked.

"I did," William said. "They beat me and fired their guns, promising to kill us." He pointed to bullets holes in the wall.

"Did you file a complaint?" Sally asked, referring to something her mother said but which Sally understood no better than Billy understood fighting back.

Tonya nodded. "William lost his job and has been out of work since then. Now we can't afford diapers or decent schools for you children."

"That sucks," Billy said.

William nodded. "It sucks hard."

Sally, remembering her manners once again, said, "Thanks for the meal. I know it's an illusion and all, but we appreciate it very much."

"You're welcome," Tonya said. "I wish there was more we could do to help."

"You can help us rescue Kitty," Billy said. "She's being held at the Kit-Kat Klub."

"That we cannot do," William said with a heavy sigh. "Even if it mattered, which it doesn't, because things are illusory, the prick-bastards Big Baby hired are walking around all over the place with guns. I'm afraid the fate of your poor kitty is beyond our control."

Billy shook his head. "No. That's not possible."

"We tried every means possible with our own beloved Kitty. It only increased our own pain and suffering. There is nothing to do."

Billy grew agitated. "What's the point of our being here if we can't rescue Kitty?"

Tonya glanced out the kitchen window. "Just talking about this can get you sent to Time Out."

"If people are that afraid of Big Baby, then it seems everybody is already in Time Out. You may as well try to save your family."

"I have an answer," William said, once again offering his sage advice. "We must find a path that causes as little trouble as possible. But when we stumble into trouble, we must then remind ourselves that all things are temporary. In the end, we all return to the earth."

"Like a cat flung from a catapult returns to the earth," Tommy said.

"That's not funny," Billy said and Billy leapt onto Tommy, punching and screaming until they were separated.

"Please Billy," Sally said. "Let's sleep and maybe we can think of something else tomorrow morning."

"That's what you always say."

"But it's all we can do."

Billy cried. "Even though I hate Mom and Dad, I wish they were here."

"I know."

Billy wiped his tears away. "Kitty is the only family we have right now. It's not right for us to sleep in peace while she rots in the Kit-Kat Klub."

During the night, Sally awoke from a disturbing dream. At home, she would have called to her mother and feigned crying until she got the attention she desired. But here she couldn't do that.

She considered waking up Billy to seek his comfort but, after their argument, she didn't think she'd find any sympathy with him.

Sally understood his concern. The only part of their plan they had accomplished was to get into town and find where the cats are imprisoned. They had found no one to help them, and taking the risk of asking Tommy's family failed. Asking another family could get them into trouble.

Maybe William was right, and finding a peaceful path was the best option.

And maybe Billy was right, and fighting to help your family was the best option.

Sally decided she had to try something. She had been upset enough to come this far to rescue Kitty. If they stopped now without trying, neither she nor Billy would ever find rest.

She crossed the room to Billy's bed, excited to tell him of her decision.

But Billy wasn't in his bed.

Sally turned on the light and searched the room, but Billy wasn't there.

Chapter Twelve

She crept through the house but she couldn't find him. Then she went back to their room and noticed that Billy's shoes and backpack were gone. So Sally dressed and went to where she was certain he must have gone.

Sally hurried through the deserted streets. Suspicious of the gas lighting and unsure of her direction, she returned to the abandoned factory-school because that was how she had learned the location of the Kit-Kat Klub. Billy would try to break Kitty out.

"You should have paid attention," she said, trying to comfort herself with criticism like her mother would offer in such a situation. But her mother's critical words, although familiar, were no more comforting now than they were when Sally had forgotten to bring along her ballet slippers for her most recent dance competition.

Sally found the school, recognizing the smell of spilled gasoline and dead skunk in the darkness even before she saw the abandoned factory. From there she went to the barbed wire fence and walked along it, searching in the darkness for any signs of Billy.

A siren wailed in the distance and Sally saw an orange glow toward Big Baby Tower. Fire! And there was a figure approaching. Billy! She recognized his gait. Without looking her way, he crossed the street, ran along the fence, and squatted down with some kind of tool.

Sally glanced around at the dark and silent houses, but no one was there. Either the sirens had not awakened them

MICKEY HADICK

or else they didn't care. Sally slipped over to where Billy crouched down. He raised the tool, ready to strike.

"It's me," Sally said. "Relax."

"Oh, sorry," Billy said.

"What are you doing?"

"Trying to cut through this fence." He squeezed wire cutters with both hands, but he couldn't make it work.

"Where did you get this stuff?"

"The pole barn by the park. I figured that's where they keep the catapult so that's where they'd keep a bunch of tools. I snagged a gas can from the so-called school for the fire, and then grabbed all this stuff from the pole barn to bust Kitty out."

"You set that fire?" Sally squeaked.

Billy shrugged. "It truly doesn't matter."

"Where did you get the idea to do all that?"

"From that television show mom and dad have been watching about the drug dealers and the cops. Between television and the internet, a kid can learn a lot of stuff."

Sally looked through the tool bag and found what seemed to be a much larger version of the wire cutters Billy held onto. "Let's try this."

Working together, they could snip through the chain link. They each grabbed a handle and carried the tool bag to huts inside the compound.

"Kitty?" Sally called.

There was a noise in the nearest hut, but in the darkness they couldn't see inside through the slotted window.

Billy went to work on the lock. "We have to let them all out, anyway."

Sally realized he was right. They couldn't leave any of the cats behind.

They struggled at first, but together they cut through the lock on the door using the long-handled snippers. When they opened the door, a cat peered back at them from inside.

But it wasn't Kitty.

"It's okay," Sally said. "We're rescuing you."

The cat blinked. "You're joking, right?"

"Nope," Billy said. "We're busting you out."

They went to the next hut and set to work on cutting the lock off. This one went a little quicker and, again, the cat inside blinked at them.

By the time they had four more huts open, the cats emerged from their huts.

One of those cats rubbed against Sally's leg. "Did you bring any food?"

"No, sorry. You're hungry?"

The cat nodded. "Big Baby likes his cats to be skinny, so they starve us."

"That's terrible," Sally said. But it also reminded her of things her mother had said to Sally about eating 'too much.'"

"It's no worse than any of the other stuff that happens in this town."

"They've all lost their minds," another cat said.

The next hut they opened revealed a cat that had already died.

"Oh no," Sally said. "I'm so sorry."

"At least she will be mourned," said the first cat. "So many have passed on without so much as a by your leave."

They came to the last hut. Lock-busting pros by now, it took only a moment to release the latch. Sally swung open the door and peered inside at the small, thin occupant.

It was Kitty.

Mickey Hadick

Chapter Thirteen

Their friend panted, eyes squeezed shut, unable to walk. Sally and Billy sat with her, cradling her in their arms, just as they had done when they first met.

"What do we do now?" Billy said.

"Let me think," Sally said.

The cats who had been freed sat and stared at them.

"Don't you have a plan?" one said.

"Sort of," Sally said. "But we were only trying to rescue Kitty. This is all very unexpected, so now we're improvising."

"I see," said the cat. "Allow me." She turned to the others and announced, "Battle plan Omega. Go!"

All the other cats slipped off into the night.

The remaining cat faced Billy and Sally again. "You will care for her?"

"Yes," Sally said. "We're family."

With that, the remaining cat turned and fled into the night.

Sally and Billy settled Kitty inside Billy's backpack and slipped out of the Kit-Kat Klub the way they had come in.

"Now what?" Billy asked.

"We need food and water for Kitty. Let's go back to Tommy's house."

They hid in the yard behind the house and agreed that Sally would go inside for supplies. Billy would run away with Kitty if anything went wrong.

As Sally foraged in the kitchen, Wendy surprised her.

MICKEY HADICK

"What are you doing?" Wendy asked.

"Looking for food."

"But why were you outside?"

"I was curious about the sirens."

Wendy nodded. "That woke me up, too. I thought maybe you and Billy tried to rescue your kitty."

"Oh, well, if we did, we'd probably not tell you so you wouldn't get in trouble for aiding and abetting."

"What does that mean?"

"I think it means you get into trouble for helping us," Sally said. "I heard it on a television show."

Wendy went to the cupboard and dug deep behind the boxed cereal. She pulled out a bag of cat food. "I saved this in case we got our own cat back. Her name was Lady Meowsalot. I called her Lady."

"Thank you," Sally said. "I'm sorry about what happened to Lady Meowsalot."

"I miss her."

Sally hugged Wendy. "I'd invite you outside to meet Kitty, but I don't want to get you into trouble."

"I don't think it'll matter," Wendy said. "So I'll go."

Kitty, nestled in Billy's arms, drank the water and ate a little food. This revived her somewhat.

"Do you have an escape plan?" Kitty whispered.

"Yes," Sally said. "Now that we found you. We have to—"

Sirens blared from all across the town. Police! The wailing sirens rose and fell as the cars turned up and down streets, but there was no mistaking that they were closing in.

"Maybe we should wait," Sally said.

"Maybe we should run," Billy said.

A police car drove along the street and swept the houses on both sides of the street with a spotlight.

"Okay, we can wait," Billy said.

SALLY AND BILLY IN BABYLAND AND THEIR ADVENTURES WITH KITTY THE CAT

William came outside and found them next to the shed. "I feared this might happen," he said. "Wendy, I need you inside. I can't bear to lose family, again."

"We're sorry," Sally said. "We'll go now."

"No. There are patrols on the street and they are going door to door. We're pretty high on their list so they'll be here soon. If they don't find you out here, come inside later and we'll figure out what to do."

Sally moved them behind the shed, further out of sight, and waited.

When the police arrived, there was no mistaking what happened. Sally heard the front door kicked in and a man shouting for the family to sit on the floor. Then all the police shouted at each other as they searched the house.

After still more shouting at each other, they moved on to the next house and kicked in that door.

"Hey," Billy whispered. "Why don't they search the back yards?"

Kitty looked left and right into the darkness. "Either they are stupid, or—"

A dog barked. Then two more dogs barked. Border patrol! While the police searched the house, the dogs searched the yards.

"I hadn't thought of this," Sally said. "Let's get inside."

"No," Kitty said, lifting her head and sniffing the air. "They're too close."

Sally peaked around the corner of the shed and two dogs were in the yard. While one sniffed around the house, the other made its way across the yard.

His sniffing quickened and he walked with purpose to the shed.

The dog had picked up their scent.

Chapter Fourteen

Sally cowered behind the shed with one arm around Billy and her other hand on Kitty, stroking her for comfort.

The dog's sniffing came closer. Then it stopped. After a minute, Sally gathered the courage to look up.

And there, within a foot of her face, was Pinscher, the dog she saved in the river.

Pinscher glared at Kitty and his lips peeled back to reveal his fangs. A low growl trembled from his throat.

"Please," Sally whispered. "Help us."

For another minute they stared at each other, Sally expecting her face to be bitten off.

"Hey," the other dog barked. "You got something?"

Pinscher released his breath and turned away. "No," he said. "Just needed a minute."

"Well lick yourself on your own time. We've got work to do."

Pinscher looked back at Sally. "Good luck," he whispered.

"Thank you."

The gun shots rang out down the street.

"Let's go," the other dog barked.

Pinscher turned and ran off into the darkness.

#

They all sat on the floor of the front room, with the lights out and the broken door barricaded with a chair.

SALLY AND BILLY IN BABYLAND AND THEIR ADVENTURES WITH KITTY THE CAT

"We're sorry to cause trouble," Sally said. "I didn't mean for anyone else to get involved."

William shrugged. "It doesn't matter."

"Maybe we could hide here for a while," Billy said. "Like that Dutch girl, Anne Frank."

"She was Jewish," Sally said.

"Whatever. That worked pretty well, hiding up in the attic."

"She was discovered and sent to a concentration camp where she died."

"Oh. I guess I should have watched the rest of the movie."

"That might work for a short while," William said, "but the brutes are angrier than usual."

"We did release all the cats," Sally said.

"And burned the catapult," Billy added.

William peeked out the front window. "It looks like we're staying right here for a while."

Sally joined him at the window. As the light of dawn spread across the neighborhood, security guards in their black diapers kept watch at every corner. Police cars cruised along the street, and border patrol dogs sniffed along each house.

"Burning the catapult kept the cops pretty busy," Billy said. "Couldn't we burn something else?"

"And then sneak out of the other side of town?" Sally added.

William shook his head. "Anybody outside their home, now, will be arrested. You won't get ten feet."

Sally plopped herself in the middle of the floor and cupped her head in her hands, tired and frustrated. "The plan was to meet Chuck and Laurie at the public toilet in the park. They would smuggle us out of town from there."

"Who are Chuck and Laurie?"

"The Canadians who unplug toilets."

MICKEY HADICK

William nodded. "There's a good chance Big Baby will hold a rally at the park. Whenever there's a problem, like a contagious disease or spoiled food, he waits a few hours and then holds a rally to blame someone and claim victory for himself."

"That makes no sense," Sally said.

"No it doesn't."

William paced back and forth for a few moments. "The trick is to join the crowd that gathers at the park without drawing too much attention to ourselves."

"We can hide Kitty in the backpack," Billy suggested.

"Backpacks get searched. It has to be something else."

Tonya hurried to her bedroom and returned in a moment wearing a maternity dress. She stuffed a pillow under the dress and she looked pregnant. "We can hide Kitty under here."

William scratched his head. "I'm the first one to admit everything is an illusion, but I wish we had a better one than that."

In the morning, the family joined the stream of people making their way on foot toward the park. From this neighborhood, only a few of the adults wore diapers.

And now, for the first time, William and Tonya wore diapers.

Tonya had torn apart their bed sheet to fashion them, leaving ample room in the rear.

Of the two, Tonya fit in with the others better, wearing a loose-fitting top above her diaper. William, however, felt the chill in the air and his skin was covered in goose bumps. He walked as if there were something clawing at him from behind.

Sally and Billy in Babyland and Their Adventures With Kitty the Cat

The family stayed close behind William, doing their best to conceal his rear end.

Kitty, of course, was along for the ride, stuffed into William's diaper.

They lingered just outside the front door, watching the stream of neighbors make their way along the road toward town.

"I sure hope this works," Billy said.

"You and me both," Kitty said.

Tonya looked down at William's rear end. "Who said that?"

"I think it was the cat," William said.

"Thank goodness," Tonya said. "I thought it was your ass."

Sally explained that cats and dogs speak. "But Kitty's not going to talk anymore, right Kitty?"

"I won't," Kitty said. "As long as William doesn't break wind."

"We'd better get going," Tonya said.

People filled the park, milling about, facing Big Baby Tower where a large podium stood in front.

Massive banners of Big Baby's head surrounded the podium. The expression on his face was a smile and a sneer —a smeer—like Sally's father's face after he farted.

Large bleachers stood next to the podium, creating a stadium effect. Men and women wearing diapers and adorned with jewelry were packed into the bleachers.

"Who is that?" Billy asked. "Why do they get to sit down?"

"Those are the rich people," William explained. "They're special."

Billy scratched his head. "They're special because they're rich, or they got rich because they're special?"

"Depends on who you ask."

They stayed on the edge of the crowd, allowing others to press forward as they came closer and closer to the public toilets.

Big Baby emerged from the tower and stood on the podium near a lectern and microphone, front and center. He looked with displeasure at the crowd gathered before him.

A tall, fat man in a diaper whispered in Big Baby's ear. The tall, fat man—his nose swollen and cheeks mottled red —reminded Sally of the principal at school who always seemed angry about something. This man had so many double chins there was no way to see his neck. But his breasts were the most disturbing, drooping low across his belly, with the nipples pointed down at the slippers on his feet.

"I wish he'd wear a shirt," Tonya whispered, shaking her head.

"Or at least a bra," Sally offered in an attempt at levity. The strain of their situation wore on her nerves, but every-one laughed.

A bald woman joined the group on the podium in front of Big Baby Tower and she also whispered something to Big Baby. It seemed her face was nothing but mouth. When she smiled, wrinkle lines appeared all over her face, reminding Sally of a shriveled apple hanging on a tree in winter.

"I'm frightened," Sally said.

"That's her specialty," William whispered. "She's just re-pulsive. There's not enough gas lighting in the world to make anyone like her."

Big Baby stepped up to the lectern and cleared his throat as he looked the audience over.

"Thank you for coming here today," he said, "on this tragic and spiteful day."

Sally didn't like the sound of his voice. It was like the bullies at school caught doing something, and desperately trying to talk their way out of trouble.

Big Baby smeered. "You see the crimes perpetrated here, especially my beloved catapult destroyed. I really loved that thing."

Big Baby looked at the crowd expectantly. "Didn't you love it?"

The crowd applauded. It was just a smattering at first, but then it caught on and grew louder.

William turned and looked at Tonya. "I have to go the bathroom."

William walked toward the men's room. Billy and Tommy followed him, following close enough behind to cover his rear.

"Thank you," Big Baby said as the applause died down. "I promise that the culprits will be brought to justice. And you know how I am about my promises. I'm great at promising things, don't you think?"

Big Baby waited for applause. Once again there was a smattering, then his assistants on the podium applauded and it caught on with the crowd.

"Thank you."

William went into the men's room while Billy and Tommy waited outside.

"We, the citizens of Babyland," Big Baby intoned from the lectern, "are rebuilding our land and restoring its promise for all of our people. We have faced challenges. We have confronted hardships. And we're getting the job done. It has been great. I really liked what we have done with the place, especially the window treatments."

William opened the door and motioned for Billy to join him inside.

MICKEY HADICK

"Today has been marred by an act of terrorism. An act of treason. It was very treasonous.

"But the loss of our catapult, and the pole barn that contained it, will not stop our progress. We will build an even bigger catapult. One that can fling multiple cats at once. I always thought we should have that, and didn't understand why it couldn't just happen. But now I'll insist. And you know I always get what I want."

William opened the door again, gave a nod to Tommy, and slipped back inside the men's room.

"And we'll build an even bigger pole barn to keep it. I want a pole barn that can hold the catapult and also my snow mobile, my four-wheeler, and my boat. And, I don't know if you know this, but I have a really big boat. It's huge. So when I tell you we need a big pole barn for all of my stuff, I'm not joking. I mean, what's the point of a pole barn if you can't put your boat in it during the off-season, am I right?

"Oh and we'll probably have to raise taxes to make that happen but I know you won't mind because things will be so awesome that you'll all be like, wow, that's awesome. You see what I'm saying? This puny act of treason, which was still very treasonous even though it pales in comparison to what I'm capable of doing, is not the point."

William emerged from the men's room and walked back toward Sally and Tonya.

"I love how the people of Babyland came together this morning, just like that one Christmas special with the green guy who stole everything. But the people he robbed didn't mind. That's how I think of you people, that no matter how much is taken away, you don't seem to mind. I love that about you.

"What matters is not that I'm in charge of this place, but that you common people come together and fix things when they break. You don't just do things, but you do what I tell you to do. I love that about you. That's what makes this place so awesome."

Sally searched for a guard.

"You want great schools for the children, safe neighborhoods for your families, and good jobs for yourselves. These are the just and reasonable demands of a righteous public. And for those of you that have them, I say, 'You're welcome.'

"But for too many of our citizens, a different reality exists: Mothers and children trapped in poverty; rusted-out factories scattered like tombstones across the landscape of our town; an education system flush with cash, but which leaves our young and beautiful students deprived of knowledge. If you think anything will be given to you for nothing, you're wrong. Very wrong. But I promise if you work hard, great things will happen. You have to work hard, though. Very hard."

Sally found a woman in a gray diaper and gray smock. The patch on her smock showed that she was a Peacekeeper for the Parks and Recreation Department. But the look on her face seemed anything but peaceful. As the guard listened to Big Baby's speech, her face twisted in anger and one side of her upper lip quivered. She didn't look away until Sally tugged on the woman's smock.

"What do you want?" the woman said.

"The men's room toilet is plugged," Sally said as she took one step back. "It's flooded, in fact."

She glared at Sally. "What do you care?"

"I think you should put an Out Of Order sign in front of the door so no one gets hurt."

The woman glanced over at the men's room. "The men can hold it."

MICKEY HADICK

"That is the past," Big Baby said. "And now we are looking only to the future. We are assembled here today because of this treasonous act of terrorism. My promise to you is that the responsible parties will pay for this. I mean that, because pole barns are very expensive when you do it right, and everybody must pay their share, especially the traitors. So I'm declaring them guilty, right here, right now. I'm not messing around.

"It wouldn't surprise me if it was one of those Canadians, by the way. I know they seem polite, but I never trusted them. No one is that polite.

"I don't know why we allow them to keep coming back in here. Do you? I'm serious. I really can't remember."

Sally tugged on the woman's smock again in frustration. "Are you going to do nothing?"

"What is your problem?"

"I think you should call someone to unplug the toilets."

"No," the woman said. "The men can just use the woman's restroom if they have to go."

Sally felt anxious. This woman needed to summon Chuck and Laurie or the plan wouldn't work.

Sally hurried to the women's room and plugged the toilets, shoving paper towels into the bowl.

Tonya came in. "Sally, what are you doing?"

"It makes no sense," Sally said as she flushed the toilets. "All the woman had to do was put up a sign and call for Chuck and Laurie."

"I know but maybe we have to find a different guard."

Sally flushed again and then stepped back as the water spilled over the bowl. "Why do people who wear diapers even use toilets?"

"They don't use them as diapers," Tonya said. "It's just for show."

With all three toilet bowls plugged and water on the floor, Sally stepped back and took a breath. "It's all so stupid."

"I know. Let's go find another guard."

Tonya opened the door, but the woman guard was standing there.

The guard looked at water on the floor and glared at Sally.

"It wasn't me," Sally said.

But the woman shoved past Tonya and grabbed Sally, dragging her away.

Chapter Fifteen

The woman leaned close to study Sally's face. Her breath smelled like one of Billy's sneakers, and Sally squirmed to get away.

"Who are you?"

"Let her go," Tonya said.

The guard looked at Tonya then put her face back in Sally's. "You're one of those runaways, ain't ya'?"

"Please," Tonya said. "You're hurting her."

Two more guards arrived, one grabbing Tonya and the other William as he rushed over.

Sally tried to get away, to kick the guard, and even to bite the guard's hand, but it was no use. She was overpowered and pulled through the crowd. The townspeople jeered at her. "Is she the one?" someone asked. "Did she do it?"

Girls shoved her and boys spat upon her. Old men slapped her behind and women yanked her hair.

The iron grip of the woman propelled Sally through the crowd. They stopped near the bleachers in front of the Police Station, and one of the security guards in a black diaper stepped up. "What have we here?"

"This one likes to plug toilets."

"Oh does she," the man in the black diaper said.

Sally looked around for Tonya or William. But only if they might help. She didn't want them to be in custody like herself.

She noticed a chant rising from the crowd. "Fuck the Canadians! Fuck the Canadians!" They repeated it over and over, louder and louder.

Sally remembered that Chuck and Laurie were Canadians and hoped they did not come to unplug the toilet. The anger she had sensed in the crowd as they jeered at her moments ago was nothing compared to the fury she sensed now.

The crowd shifted and moved with the chant, "Fuck the Canadians." From where she stood, she couldn't see what was going on, but something was going on.

"Have you always hated the Canadians?" She asked the security officer.

"No, not always," he said. "It was blacks first, then Mexicans and Muslims, but they're all gone."

"Gone? Gone where?"

The security officer shrugged. "Time out?"

There was more Sally wanted to ask but it didn't matter once she saw what was happening in the crowd. Some portion of the crowd had formed a mob and now appeared to be dragging something. The mob approached the steps of Big Baby Tower and made a circle around what they had dragged.

It was Chuck and Laurie, beaten, bloody...dead.

Chapter Sixteen

"Oh God," Sally said, and sat down hard. She sobbed and retched.

"Fucking Canadians," the security officer muttered.

Sally looked at him with bewildered horror. What manner of savage animal would say only that having seen what they saw? But then she was surrounded by hundreds of savage animals, and they cheered each other in their semicircle around what remained of Chuck and Laurie.

"You know what I call two dead Canadians?" Big Baby boomed over the PA system. "A good start."

The crowd roared with celebratory fury, clenching their fists in the air as they cheered.

Shaking off the terror of Chuck's eye dangling from its socket and Laurie's jaw twisted into a grotesque smirk, Sally's chest tightened as she realized their plan was broken. That she, Billy, and Kitty would have to escape from Babyland some other way. If they could escape, that is. Then she felt guilty for even thinking about her own problems when Chuck and Laurie had been destroyed for no other reason than being Canadian.

Billy. Where was Billy?

Across the park, a crowd had gathered around the public restroom.

Men in the crowd kicked and pounded on the men's room door. They made way as a security detail arrived with a battering ram and slammed into the door.

The door shattered open and the mob poured in.

Sally heard Kitty's growl but it was drowned out by the roar of the mob as it swarmed at Kitty, closing in and dog-piling the doomed cat.

The mob parted for a moment and there were Billy and Tommy, held with their arms pinned behind their backs by grown men. A black bag was pulled over Billy's head, then another over Tommy's.

A black bag was pulled over her own head. She would die soon. She, Billy, and Tommy. She was sure of it.

And maybe that was not such a bad thing.

Chapter Seventeen

Big Baby had the top three floors of the tower to himself. The bottom of those three were his offices, half for his business office, half for his government office, with support staff and security for both.

Every inch of the walls of the support staff area displayed motivational posters featuring Big Baby, all variations on the theme, "You can be awesome... If you try hard enough."

In here, there was no escaping Big Baby.

The next floor up was a living space with a sitting area, a dining area, large kitchen, movie theater, and a bar. The walls displayed pictures and paintings of Big Baby—Big Baby with some man, Big Baby golfing, Big Baby boating. The most curious pictures were of Big Baby with various cats. The pictures were lined up, side by side, along one wall. In each of the cat pictures, Big Baby looked into the camera while holding a cat—always with both hands and often with both arms wrapped around the cat.

The top floor was Big Baby's private chamber. Only a very select set of people other than Big Baby ever went to the top floor of Big Baby Tower.

All of this was described to Sally as part of her orientation, to explain to her the many things she was not supposed to do. For instance, she was not supposed to pay attention to any conversations taking place in or around the offices. She was not supposed to read any papers she came across. And she was not to discuss any aspects of what she did in the offices with anyone except her immediate supervisor. Most of all, she was not to go any place in the building unless she was told to go there by her immediate supervisor.

That was fine with Sally. She only wanted a few things in life at this moment, and chief among those was to not go to Big Baby's private chamber on the top floor.

On the third floor from the top, in the security area, Sally was processed, informed of her situation and given a pale green smock to wear. "You are a declared visitor with undesignated status," the security officer said.

"What if I was undeclared?" she asked.

"You would have been sent to Time Out."

"What happened to that boy taken from the restroom?"

"Just do your job or you'll find out."

Sally was delivered into the care of the stern, repulsive woman with the big mouth who had been on the steps with Big Baby during the speech. The fear and dislike of the woman Sally felt earlier intensified in her presence.

"My name is Elle, and you can call me Ms. Elle."

Sally nodded.

"Come with me."

Sally was shown to a broom closet and ordered to pick up a bucket and cleaning implements.

"What am I to do?"

"You are to scrub and clean toilets at first. We'll see how that goes."

There were several restrooms on that floor. None of them, it seemed, had been cleaned in a while. The toilets were disgusting. Considering so many people wore diapers, you would think the toilets would be spotless.

And it turned out that Sally was terrible at cleaning toilets.

"Is this how your mother taught you?" Ms. Elle said, watching as Sally struggled to even grip the scrub brush.

"I guess my mom never showed me how."

Ms. Elle shook her head. "Typical. So you grew up in filth and disarray."

"No," Sally said. "My mom paid someone else to clean."

"I see," the woman said. Sally thought the sternness in Ms. Elle's expression softened.

Sally figured out how to scrub the floor and clean the toilets. The first restroom took what seemed to be several hours. Her knees were rubbed raw and her neck and shoulders were sore from the exertion. When at last it was done, she hoped she might have a snack and rest.

"Don't be stupid," Ms. Elle said. "You're here to work. Besides, you look like you could stand to lose a few pounds."

"That's just mean," Sally said.

"Do you understand that you are being punished for whatever you did wrong?"

Sally shook her head. "I didn't do anything wrong. I was caught trying to help. But it seems that, because I don't have my parents with me, I'm being exploited."

Ms. Elle chuckled. "We hear that complaint a lot. People say it's unfair that their circumstances made them poor, or it's not their fault they got sick, and so they want help. But we believe if you're poor or you get sick, the best thing we can do is put you to work."

"But how does that help?"

"Recognize that good fortune comes when opportunity meets preparation. The opportunity we offer is a chance to work very hard, like digging holes or scrubbing toilets. The preparation is a willingness to work very hard at the same thing for a long time. That way, anyone may succeed."

"I think that just traps people into doing something unpleasant, and makes the sick get sicker and die."

"You haven't considered their lack of alternatives."

"Maybe you've been exposed to gas lighting for too long."

"Excuse me?"

"Doesn't gas lighting cloud your mind so you're not sure what's real and what's true?"

Ms. Elle smiled. "That has never been proven."

"I'm not surprised," Sally said. "You've been sniffing gas light for years."

Ms. Elle's smile disappeared. She slapped Sally across the cheek.

Sally turned and cringed in pain.

"This will be a lesson in your alternatives," Ms. Elle said, and slapped Sally across the other cheek.

Security officers who'd been standing by bent Sally over and Ms. Elle beat the back of Sally's legs with the broom.

And Sally cried until she screamed.

Chapter Eighteen

After the beating, they locked Sally in a small room in the basement and left her there for the night. She cried and yelled for help, but no one came to help her.

In the morning, a security officer took her back to the office area.

Ms. Elle glared at Sally. "Are you ready to take advantage of your opportunity and work very hard?"

Sally nodded.

She scrubbed and cleaned toilet after toilet, restroom after restroom.

Around the time Sally completed her work, Big Baby entered the office.

Up close, Sally realized how wearing nothing but slippers and a diaper revealed his age. His breasts sagged and jiggled as he moved. There were brown and red blotches scattered all over his skin. The hanging jowls of his cheeks blended into the folds of his neck. And his ears, which seemed too big for his head, had thick tufts of hair sprouting.

Everyone in the office gathered around for an announcement.

"I'd like to thank you for coming to work," he said. "Yesterday was a great day, don't you think?"

Big Baby looked around at the office workers and security staff. He nodded and smiled until there was applause.

"Thank you," he said. "I like to think these difficult decisions are the correct decisions. No one has ever told me I was wrong. Not once, and I think that's significant."

Again, he nodded and smiled until there was applause.

"Thank you. I'd like to point out I don't condone violence. It's bad. Sometimes people get hurt because of violence. But sometimes it's necessary to get your way."

Big Baby stood a little taller as he looked at those gathered around him.

"I think the people of this town needed to blow off a little steam. I know I do every once in a while."

Big Baby lifted his right leg and pretended to fart, waving his hand for ventilation. Then he gaped at the crowd and smiled, and he got the laughter he sought.

"Thank you. In all seriousness, in light of the disturbances yesterday, I've declared Canadians an enemy of our people. Any remaining Canadians in town are to be expelled. Any Canadians attempting to resist expulsion or to gain entry to our town will go to Time Out. Any Canadians found malingering in the areas surrounding our town may be killed."

Big Baby nodded and smiled, waiting for applause.

"I think that's fair."

Big Baby seemed about to disperse them but then he added, "One more thing. I'd like to introduce you to my new cat."

Two security officers entered. One of them held Kitty in his arms and presented her to Big Baby. The other carried a small cage.

Kitty's eyes were open but she was listless, her breathing seemed labored and Sally wanted nothing more than to check on her. Something was the matter. But Sally didn't dare.

MICKEY HADICK

Big Baby took hold of Kitty by the scruff of the neck and shook her. "That's my new girl," he said. "She's got spunk, this one. We'll see how long she lasts, though." He dropped Kitty back into the officer's arms and went into his office without another look back.

Then the security officers caged Kitty and took her away before Sally could get a closer look.

"Where are they taking her?" Sally asked.

"That pathetic excuse for a cat will have the privilege of living upstairs in the private chambers of Big Baby."

"He won't hurt her, will he?"

Elle took a deep breath and squared her shoulders. "What he does to that cat is none of your beeswax. She will have the honor of giving her life to bring pleasure to the greatest man who ever lived."

Chapter Nineteen

Ms. Elle became Sally's only companion. And Ms. Elle grew harsher as each day passed, seeming to grow tired of Sally.

"You're getting worse at your job," the woman said. "Maybe I should send you to Time Out and be done with it. What do you say to that?"

Sally, doing all she could to please her and last long enough until she could find a way out of this mess, apologized. "You've been patient with me, so thank you."

Sally disliked having to say such things, but it was the only comment that didn't get her rations cut or her ears boxed.

The woman smoothed her smock top. "No more lollygagging."

Sally longed for the company of her mother, in spite of her mother's critical comments and frustrated exclamations. At least with her mother, Sally could lash out and spend quality time yelling at each other until they both cried.

Here, with this stern woman, Sally knew that her next harsh utterance to the woman would also be her last. And to shed tears before this woman would mean a black bag over Sally's head and a trip to Time Out.

About this Sally was torn. She was desperate to know what had happened to Billy. But she wanted to stay close to Kitty in case there was an opportunity for them to escape.

At these moments, Sally longed for her mother more than anything. Trying to make so many important decisions

MICKEY HADICK

had exhausted her. And none of them worked out the way she hoped. She knew she was terrible at it.

Ms. Elle's constant picking didn't help, either.

Even at the end of her day, when the sun had set and Sally was given a satchel of food to eat alone in her room, there was only acrimony from the woman. "Let's see if you can at least figure out how to fall asleep without screwing that up."

The next day, Ms. Elle pulled Sally aside before she'd started scrubbing.

Ms. Elle leaned close to Sally's ear and whispered. "You wouldn't talk about me to anyone, would you?"

Sally smelled the eggs and stale coffee on her breath. "No. There's nothing to say."

"Good. Remember that, and you might just live until tomorrow."

Ms. Elle stood back up, nodded, and then a black bag came down over Sally's head.

When the bag was removed from her head, Sally stood in an empty room with bare walls and two bright lights in the ceiling.

A few feet away from her sat Mr. E on the room's only furniture, a metal folding chair. "Do you know who I am?" he asked.

Sally nodded.

"Do you know where you are?"

Sally did not.

"This is the processing center for Time Out. I'll ask you a few questions. Depending on your answers, you may go back to your place scrubbing toilets in Big Baby Tower. Or you may go through the door behind you into Time Out."

Sally glanced over her shoulder, her eyes welling with tears. She didn't want to cry but the confusion had gotten to her and she wished very much she could just hide in her room knowing her parents were in the house. Even if her parents were arguing and would argue forever more, she wanted to be with them rather than here.

Mr. E pointed at the door. "Open it. I want you to see what's there. Then I'll ask my questions. Go on."

Sally, her knees trembling, shuffled across the room. She turned the knob and opened the door.

Outside there was a barren, dusty field. There were people sitting and standing in the field, each one of them with a black bag over their head. It was difficult to tell men from women, boys from girls.

There were also two people, she thought they were boys, collapsed on the ground.

Sally looked back at Mr. E.

"They don't spend every minute of every day like that. They also are confined to huts, alone, where they sleep. And we put them to work. Do you want to go to Time Out?"

Sally shook her head.

"Then close the door."

Standing before Mr. E once again, Sally could not keep herself from sobbing. Billy and Tommy were out there. Unless they were already dead.

"Do you like what you're doing, scrubbing toilets at Big Baby's Tower?"

Sally did not, but she nodded. "Yes."

"Do you wish any harm to come to Big Baby?"

Sally did, but she shook her head. "No."

Mr. E nodded. "Just one more question: has Ms. Elle said anything about me? Not just to you, but have you overheard anything in the office? I would be very grateful if you would tell me. In fact, I would make things much better for you."

MICKEY HADICK

Maybe the gas lighting had gotten to her and she was losing touch with reality, but now all that Sally wanted was to go back to scrubbing toilets. She was just a little kid. How could she know what game Mr. E wanted her to play?

Maybe it would be better to just wait until she was old enough to put on a diaper and try to fit in.

"No," Sally said. "I have heard nothing about you."

Chapter Twenty

A few days later, as Sally dragged a bucket of filthy water out of a restroom, standing before her in a green smock of her own was Wendy.

Ms. Elle gave Sally a shove. "Show her where things are and I'll be along presently."

Once they were alone in the broom closet, Wendy smiled. "It's nice to see you."

"I wasn't sure you remembered me," Sally said.

"Don't let on that you know me," Wendy whispered. "Elle won't like that."

"No she won't. What are you doing here?"

"I volunteered so I could talk to you."

"What is there to talk about?" Sally asked. "There's no point to anything. None of this. Nothing."

Wendy peeked out the door to check that they were alone. "But there is a big change about to happen. We need to get out of this tower."

"Why? Aren't we all going to die, anyway? Is there no point to any of this?"

"There isn't any point. And yes we're all going to die."

Sally grabbed a bucket and scrub brush and offered it to Wendy. "So let's do what we have to do and not worry any more."

"We were wrong about the nihilism. There are too many people and cats suffering. Standing by idly because there's no point is not the best option."

Wendy checked the door again. "Your acts of defiance have inspired many people. The Kit-Kat Klub, the pole barn, and the plugged toilets changed things."

Sally was skeptical. She'd seen a vast crowd of normal people turn into savage animals who attacked innocent people. A big, stupid baby who only cared about himself led the mob, and anybody that resisted them went to Time Out. "Let me do my job."

Wendy shook her head. "By tomorrow, everything will be very different."

"What could be different?"

"Bullets. There will be a lot of shooting going on."

Sally shook her head. "Maybe that's for the best."

Before Wendy could say anything else, Elle returned and took her to a restroom on the other side of the building, leaving Sally to continue where she left off.

There was a foul smell inside, but she was used to her lot in life and settled in to clean.

Ever since the visit to Time Out, she'd been trapped in this building, working by day, locked inside a room each night with no chance to escape, and no hope for things to get better. But she thought it was what she deserved. It was all her fault they were in the situation they were in. She should have been a better kid so that Mom and Dad hadn't left her and Billy in the woods.

Sally finished scrubbing the toilets but the foul smell remained. She searched the stalls and found a dirty diaper behind one toilet. She'd so focused on the commodes she hadn't noticed it wedged between the toilet and the wall.

It was a doozie. The mess had overflowed and dragging it out into view smeared the floor and wall with more mess.

Disgusted and frustrated, Sally cried. This should not be her mess to clean up. This was a mistake by a pathetic excuse for an adult.

These people were bad enough already, wearing diapers for fashion but not using them as diapers. At least they could use a toilet bowl without spilling. None of them ever had to clean a toilet in their life, and they cared nothing for those who cleaned them.

But today, someone had crapped themselves and hidden the evidence, thinking the Shit Fairy would leave them a dollar in exchange.

Adults should be able to do one thing well, and that's to keep from pooping themselves. Sally would never think less of a person who wore a diaper through no fault of their own. But wearing a diaper and using it to relieve themselves when you could perfectly use a toilet was a bad idea. A terrible idea.

Scrubbing their toilets and cleaning up their messes would not help this world. It wasn't helping these people. And it wasn't helping Billy, Kitty, or herself.

And Sally was tired of doing it.

Sally got back on her feet and dropped her scrub brush. She washed the filth from her hands and tidied herself up as best she could given the circumstances.

Then she moved her yellow, "Wet Floor" sign out of the way and stepped out of the restroom.

Whatever happened next, she would try something different. Maybe she'd make a little mess of her own.

And getting Kitty away from that big baby was a good place to start.

Chapter Twenty-One

Sally crossed through the office area to the restroom where Wendy scrubbed the floor on her hands and knees. Ms. Elle stood just outside, her arms crossed, looking in.

"Excuse me," Sally said. "But I need to get the keys so I can go upstairs to Big Baby's private rooms."

Elle scoffed. "You impertinent little slug. Do you need to go to Time Out?"

"No ma'am. It's just that Mr. E told me to do it. He said Big Baby wants his diaper changed right away and that I was to go upstairs and do it."

"Why didn't he take you there himself?"

"He said his time was too valuable, and that you should do it."

"Excuse me?"

"Yes ma'am. I know you're busy too so I thought I could just go do it. But he said these damn kids were your idea and that you should be the one to deal with it. He was busy."

"That son of a bitch," Elle said and stormed off.

Wendy stepped out of the restroom. "That was good."

"I learned it at home," Sally said. "But I hoped she would give me those keys. So now what?"

"What do you mean?"

"What's the plan?"

Wendy shrugged. "We run away."

"But that won't work. There are security officers at every door. We must be escorted in and out. We need those keys."

SALLY AND BILLY IN BABYLAND AND THEIR ADVENTURES WITH KITTY THE CAT

Sally looked around. At each desk, the adults, all of them wearing diapers, looked bored. It wasn't all that different from being in school. Maybe the only thing you learned at school was to sit at a desk and not get caught picking your nose. She used to think getting caught farting at school was the worst possible thing but, now she'd seen so very many adults wearing nothing but diapers, she was certain farting wasn't a big deal.

Ms. Elle was in Mr. E's office, their argument heard across the floor. And there were security men at the doors and the elevator. It was like her school back home. Once school started, the doors were locked and hall monitors— parents who volunteered to stand guard because they were worried about a shooter attacking the school—were at every corner and doorway. There was no way out until the end of school. Except...

An idea formed in her mind.

"How do you get people out of school all at the same time?" Sally asked.

"I don't know," Wendy said. "How?"

"A fire alarm."

"Fire alarm? What's that?"

Sally realized that they may not have done such things at the abandoned factory where Wendy went to school. "It's a pretend fire. The alarm is pulled. It's a chance to practice evacuating the school in case of a real fire. And kids love it because none of us want to be in school. We get a chance to be outside. And everybody has to leave the building."

"Okay, what do we do?"

Sally looked around and noticed the fire alarm thing on the wall over by the security area. "We pull that thing and then everybody gets up and leaves."

"Good because I think this building will blow up soon."

"What?"

MICKEY HADICK

"I don't know but I think that's what I overheard. You know how adults never explain things to kids. They told me to hurry."

Sally wanted to get more information but Wendy took off running, headed straight for the fire alarm. Sally hadn't meant for Wendy to do it herself but maybe that didn't matter either. In fact, this was better, because the rest of Sally's plan was to run up the stairs during the evacuation and make sure that Kitty was set free.

A siren screamed and pulsed, on and off and on again while lights near the exits flashed. The security officers standing guard looked around but didn't move. All the men and women stopped what they were doing and looked around.

At school, when a fire alarm goes off, the kids hurry outside because they all would rather do anything other than sit in a classroom. But here, nobody headed for the doors. Sally didn't think for even a second that these people wanted to be here. So why did they stay at their desks?

And then the answer popped into her mind. These were old people, like her parents were old. And old people get set in their ways. She understood from watching her parents stay in a marriage neither one wanted to stay in that, once you get to a certain age, you'll keep doing what you hate and staying where you don't want to be.

Old people would rather be miserable in the familiar than take a risk with something new.

The security officers grabbed Wendy and made her stand in the corner while Ms. Elle and Mr. E were summoned from his office. They were still arguing as they approached the scene, but Ms. Elle slapped Wendy, knocking her to the ground.

"Get up," she said.

Wendy got up. "Please don't hit me," she said. "I'm just a little kid." Then she threw her arms around Ms. Elle and pulled her close.

Ms. Elle, baffled by the gesture, ordered the security officers to pry Wendy off.

She and Mr. E. argued about who would punish Wendy. They decided to take turns, and slapped her across the face, hitting her until she wailed in pain and her legs collapsed. The security officers held her up so the beatings could continue.

Sally wished these fools could suffer. None of them deserved her sympathy. Not Ms. Elle, nor Mr. E. Not the security forces, nor the fools in diapers who wouldn't leave their desks to stop a little girls' suffering. She wanted nothing more than to see all of them burn, but how could she start a real fire?

The gas lights.

If she put out the flames the gas would keep hissing out of the nozzle, like a gas stove she saw in a movie once. If she put out a bunch of them, then enough of the gas might gather up to start a bigger fire.

Sally grabbed the bucket full of dirty water from the restroom, and the long handled toilet brush, and used that to throw water at the gas lights burning along the wall.

And it worked. She figured out how to dip and snap the brush in one motion, flinging enough water at the fixture to extinguish the flame. Sure enough, the gas kept hissing even though it wasn't burning.

She worked her way around the room, extinguishing gas light after gas light. She wasn't sure how many she needed to put out, so she decided to keep going until someone noticed. But no one noticed.

They were all watching Ms. Elle and Mr. E beat Wendy. They seemed to relish it like entertainment, sort of like how

MICKEY HADICK

her father watched mixed martial arts fighting on television, or her mother went shopping on Black Friday.

With the alarm silenced and the flashing lights near the exits turned off, the room grew darker as Sally had extinguished over half of the lights.

At last, Wendy's beating stopped, and Sally walked up next to her.

"Would it be all right if I take her to her room? I'll come right back and finish scrubbing."

"Fine," Ms. Elle said, breathing hard from the exertion.

"I'd like to take the stairs if that's okay. I don't want to get blood in the elevator."

"I don't care what you do."

Sally surprised herself next by maneuvering Wendy onto her back and lifting her up. She asked the security officer to open the door to the stairwell.

Before she left, she worried about what might happen to the people in the office area. She cursed her weakness, and wondered if she might be too soft to save herself from this situation. But she noticed how the fools staggered back to their desks to return to work, oblivious to the gas filling the room, and unconcerned that so many lights had gone out. They were like everybody else in the world, including her parents, who became caught up in the drama of their own, pathetic lives, that it was all they could do to get through a day.

Maybe they didn't all deserve to burn.

"I think there's something wrong with the gas lights," she said to the security officer. "You should get everybody to leave because there might be a fire."

Then Sally carried Wendy out of the office area into the stair well.

Sally and Billy in Babyland and Their Adventures With Kitty the Cat

Chapter Twenty-Two

Sally climbed up the stairs. The hard work of the past several days must have strengthened her muscles, as she carried Wendy to the top floor without much difficulty.

Then she heard an explosion. Screams from below echoed through the stairwell.

Sally set Wendy down on the landing outside the door to Big Baby's private chamber, comforting her as best she could, but there wasn't much she could do.

Sally pressed her ear to the door. "I hear the television, but that's it."

Wendy pulled a small set of keys from her pocket. "Try these," she mumbled.

"Keys? Where did you get them?"

"I picked Ms. Elle's pocket when I grabbed her to beg for mercy."

"Nice."

Sally opened the door and propped Wendy up as they went inside.

Big Baby's private chamber was as plush and regal as described in orientation. In fact, it was the nicest living space she had ever seen, in spite of the mess scattered across the floor.

It was so messy that Sally worried she wouldn't be able to see Kitty.

"What do you want?" Big Baby said. He was on his bed at one end of the chamber. Above the bed, hanging from the ceiling, was a television. On the ceiling was a mirror.

SALLY AND BILLY IN BABYLAND AND THEIR ADVENTURES WITH KITTY THE CAT

"Oh, uh..."

Big Baby scrutinized Sally. "Did you bring my bottle? All this noise woke me from my nap and I'm thirsty."

"Ms. Elle told me to come up here and get Kitty."

"What for?"

"Because of the fire. She didn't want you to worry about her."

Big Baby shrugged. "Fine." Big Baby roused himself from the bed, rolling to one side and sliding off, then pressing against the bed to stand up.

"This is all my stuff," Big Baby said. "So don't take anything. In fact, don't touch anything."

"I'll just get Kitty and go."

This chamber seemed to take up the entire top floor. At one end was the large bed, a toilet, and a bath. At the other end was a large television, a sofa, and a rocking chair. And scattered in between were hundreds of things—clean diapers, dirty diapers, little ceramics figurines that might be precious keepsakes or that might be toys. There were stacks of comic books and stacks of coloring books.

And on the walls were portraits of Big Baby. Big Baby walking in the park. Big Baby splashing in a lake. Big Baby riding a bike. Big Baby playing with a ball.

"Do you have friends up here to play very often?" Sally regretted saying it, as Big Baby turned and glared.

"I don't need friends," Big Baby said. "I have everything I need here and friends isn't one of them. So keep your grubby paws off of my stuff."

Sally lowered her gaze, as she did with Ms. Elle. "If you'll just show me Kitty, I'll be going."

"She's over there," Big Baby said, pointing to the far corner.

As Sally walked over, he followed close behind. "You don't look so smart," Big Baby said. "You're not old enough

Mickey Hadick

to wear a diaper, so how smart could you be. And you're a girl and girls aren't that smart to begin with. I bet you don't have as much stuff as I do. Well do you?"

"No I don't."

Kitty seemed weak, almost as weak as when they first met, but she had been watching from the cage as Sally approached and perked up.

"Hello," Kitty whispered. "I'm glad to see you."

"Me too. But no fighting. We have to go."

"What's that?" Big Baby asked.

"Nothing," Sally said. "I was just talking to the cat."

"That cat is mine. They all belong to me and no one else can have them. That's fine because all cats love only me, anyway."

As Sally opened the cage and lifted Kitty out and into her arms, Big Baby watched her carefully.

"Will you come back soon?" Big Baby asked. His anger was gone for a moment, and his face looked as sad as he sounded. "If not today, maybe tomorrow?"

Wendy held the door open. But as Sally stepped through, Big Baby made a small noise and Sally glanced back.

"Will you?" he asked again.

Sally realized how lonely he must be, spending so much time in his tower, letting no one in and never sharing his toys. She never, ever wanted to see this terrible person again in her life, but she didn't have the heart to tell him that. To be rejected at this moment would crush his soul.

She decided that perhaps it would be best to vaguely nod, the way adults agree to do things they never intend to do. But even as she nodded, he was distracted and didn't notice.

Big Baby was adjusting his diaper, which must have come loose while he was lying down. "I need help."

Sally and Wendy exchanged a look but said nothing.

"I order you to change my diaper," Big Baby said. "I'm in charge and you have to do what I say."

"No," Sally said. "I don't want to get anywhere near you or your diaper. You're an adult. I'm just a kid."

"But look it won't attach." Big Baby grabbed at the sticky attachment but the diaper fell off, exposing himself to Kitty and the girls.

Sally and Wendy hurried through the door.

"Wait," Big Baby said as the girls and Kitty went out the door. "What am I supposed to do?"

Kitty, snuggled innocently in Sally's arms, raised her head and said, "Take that little-bitty thing between your legs and go fuck yourself."

Chapter Twenty-Three

Sally paused on the landing. Smoke swirled around the stairs, circling upwards. Down below them, an explosion shook the metal steps beneath their feet. Screams and shouting echoed against the walls, and smoke billowed up the stairwell.

Sally coughed but took a step down. "I don't want to go down these stairs, but I think it's our only hope."

"Wait," Kitty said. "Have you seen any cats around town?"

"I have," Wendy said. "That's why I'm here. A cat visited us last night to ask for help rescuing you two."

"But why you?" Sally said, coughing.

"We're known sympathizers because of Lady Meowsa-lot."

Kitty perked up. "It's Battle Plan Omega! Go to the roof and let's hope for an airlift."

The idea was no crazier than anything else so they went up the last flight of stairs to the roof.

She was coughing and her eyes stung from the smoke, but once she was up on the roof Sally was overwhelmed with relief.

The sky was blue and the sun was bright. Up this high, they were above the stench of rotting trash and dirty dia-pers, and beyond the reach of the gas lighting. She breathed her first fresh air in a long time, and a breeze tickled her nose with the scent of pine.

Kitty jumped out of Sally's arms and ran to the edge of the building where she scouted the surrounding areas. She waved a paw.

"What is it?" Sally asked as she and Wendy joined Kitty at the edge of the roof.

Kitty pointed at a thicket of trees beyond the trench surrounding the town. "There's our ride."

Sally and Wendy tried to see who it was. They waved their hands.

Sally couldn't quite comprehend what she was seeing but she thought she saw three cats flying jet-powered planes.

They flew in a triangle formation with one jet on point and two behind, coming in low over the trench encircling the town and skimming over the house tops.

As they approached Big Baby tower, shots rang out. The soldiers from the buildings at either end of the bridge were positioning themselves in the town park and firing at the jet-powered cats.

"Me-ow," Kitty said.

More troops spilled out of the buildings, firing as they ran at the jet-powered cats. From across the trench, cats on the ground stormed the bridge. As the troops opened fired, thousands of bright lights flashed from the cats.

"What is that?" Sally asked, her heart racing at the sight of the battle.

"Lasers," Kitty said. "Each cat has a double-barreled laser gun capable of firing 40 mega-joules of death with the twitch of an ear."

"Holy crap," Sally said. "I never would have guessed cats have such technology."

"Indeed," Kitty said. "We figured emancipation from the humans wouldn't come easy. Jets and lasers seemed like table stakes."

The three jet-cats, still drawing fire, circled the top of the building, hovered and then lowered down for a landing.

While Kitty greeted and conferred with the jet-cats, Sally marveled at the machines and the domestic short hairs piloting them. There was nothing cuter in the world than a cat wearing goggles and riding a miniature jet-powered fighter plane.

Then a fourth jet approached and landed. This one apparently autonomous because it had no pilot. It was for Kitty!

Kitty jumped into the cockpit in a single bound and explained to Wendy how to help strap her in. The last thing to go on were the cute little goggles over Kitty's eyes.

"Awww," Sally said, feeling as if her heart might burst. "This is ridiculously cute and I can't even take a picture."

"Tragic," Kitty said, shaking her head. "I'd almost forgotten that cat pictures are a mainstay of human culture."

Kitty winked through her goggles and started her jet engine.

"How do you fly that thing?" Wendy asked.

"Same as any flying machine," Kitty said. "Roll, pitch, and yaw. But the downward thrust provides lift. Once we're strapped in, each paw controls a flying mechanism. The laser cannons are voice-controlled, and we use our tail to communicate to each other."

"What about us?" Sally asked, shouting over the engines.

"Put on a harness because we're carrying you out of here."

"While they're shooting at us?"

"We didn't just pick a little cat fight," Kitty said. "This is war. We are about to impose our will on the diaper-wearing, hairless apes of Baby Town."

The next moment, several flights of jet-cats emerged from behind the stand of trees and strafed the troops in the park defending the bridge.

"That should do it," Kitty said.

Sally and Wendy helped each other don the harness, no more complicated than a seat belt on a booster seat.

Wendy checked her tow cables and gave a thumbs-up.

Sally checked her tow cables and also gave a thumbs-up.

The jet-cats opened their thrusters and floated up off of the roof, lifting Sally and Wendy with them, who each dangled between two of the hovering jet planes.

Then the jet-cats fired their engines, and they sped off into the sky and out over the battlefield.

Chapter Twenty-Four

They were whisked at high speed over the town. Sally felt herself screaming but she could only hear the roar of the jet engines.

Squadron after squadron of jet-cats passed beneath them on their attack runs, flying in a V-formation, strafing the diaper-clad soldiers.

As they flew over the trench bordering the town, Sally saw that the cats had secured one end of the bridge and were advancing across it. Cats also swarmed across the trench, leaping from one pile of debris to another, sneaking behind the soldiers on the other side.

It was a bad day for the soldiers of Baby Town. Even Sally could tell that they were harassed from above and from below, and from the front, the side, and the rear. Cats were everywhere and too quick to target.

Sally and Wendy were taken to the meadow on the far side of the stand of trees where, they soon discovered, a base had been established overnight. It turned out the cats weren't doing all this on their own, but were assisted by a small army of men and women.

These soldiers wore proper uniforms—no diapers!—of drab green fatigues emblazoned with red and white maple leaf patches. Canadians!

Sally and Wendy were taken to the battle commander, an obese, long-haired cat, perched on a folding chair. She looked at the girls with eyes that blazed from the dark gray fur on her face.

"I am General Bigglesworth," the cat said.

"Like from that movie?" Sally asked.

The general shook her head. "Bigglesworth is a proud family name. Its exploitation in an inane film is not unlike the exploitation of felines throughout the ages. But that changes today."

"I meant no harm."

General Bigglesworth yawned. "I understand you helped to trigger the battle."

"I suppose. But I was just trying to help Kitty."

"And I was just trying to help Sally," Wendy said.

Sally remembered Billy. "My brother," she cried. "What happened to him? And what happened to Tommy?"

"They were both sent to Time Out," Wendy said.

"We have to save them."

General Bigglesworth was looking at a bird in a nearby tree. But once the bird flitted away, Bigglesworth turned her head and shouted, "General McKenzie!"

The Canadian general approached and saluted.

"What is the status of Time Out?"

"Fierce resistance around a fortified bunker with heavy armaments," the general said.

"Divert air support to assault that bunker. Establish a line across the town park to protect the flank, and all other troops are to assist liberating Time Out."

Chapter Twenty-Five

From the relative safety of the command post, Sally and Wendy could do nothing more than wait and worry.

Time Out was on the other side of town. They could hear the jet-cats and the laser cannons and the gun shots as the battle intensified.

Big Baby Tower was under control of the Feline-Canadian forces. Smoke billowed from the shattered windows of the top floors, and Sally wondered if Big Baby found a way out.

If this was a movie, the bad guy would try to escape. So she looked away from where the battle raged at a quiet part of Baby Town. Sure enough, a group of people in diapers made their way toward the trench.

"General Bigglesworth," Sally said, and pointed at the group.

Bigglesworth, who had been licking herself at the moment, looked up and blinked. "Me-ow," she said. "I wonder who that could be."

A detachment of Canadian troops engaged the group, charging directly at them.

But the fools in diapers were Big Baby's elite security detail, and even Sally noticed how they coordinated their defense. The fighting intensified, forcing the Canadians back.

The command post came under fire, and Sally and Wendy joined the retreat. Only the return of the jet-cats subdued the diaper-clad attackers.

At last the fighting was over.

Sally and Wendy both could see Big Baby, naked except for slippers, his hands zip-tied together, holding a diaper over his itty-bitty privates. He and Ms. Elle and Mr. E were under guard near the command post.

General McKenzie reported that Time Out had been liberated, and the detainees were being trucked back to the Command Center along with the casualties.

Sally and Wendy hurried to search for their brothers when the trucks arrived. Sally found Billy, and helped him limp over to the aid station.

When he'd had water and a snack, Billy lifted his head and asked, "Where's Kitty?"

Sally pointed to the sky.

"You mean she died?" Billy said.

"No. She's jetting around, fighting the diaper-soldiers."

"She is such a good kitty."

"Where's Tommy?" Sally asked.

Billy shook his head. "He didn't make it."

"What?"

From across the field, they heard Wendy scream in deep anguish. She was at the last of the trucks, and they had just carried Tommy's body out and laid him on the ground.

Sally sat down next to Billy and cried. She cried for Tommy, the unselfish boy who had helped her. And she cried in anger at the selfish man who wore a diaper and acted like a child, causing harm to so many. And she cried in befuddlement that the world allowed such things to come to pass.

"Tommy asked me to tell you something," Billy said. "Even though our so-called reality is only an illusion conjured by our brain's interpretation of the senses, he was glad he met you. And the way you cared for Kitty and your family made him realize that taking care of each other matters. And he was glad he helped us."

MICKEY HADICK

It took a moment for Sally to process Tommy's message. And then she cried even harder, sorry that she couldn't thank Tommy or maybe give him a hug.

A commotion broke out near the command post. Mr. E, the hideous adviser to Big Baby, had escaped with a bomb and charged at them, a terrible look of angry desperation on his face, dead set on destroying what he couldn't control.

As he bore down on Sally and Billy, the roar of a jet-cat drowned out their screams. The bomb exploded, throwing Sally backwards and slamming her to the ground.

Everything went black.

Chapter Twenty-Six

Sally awoke, cold and on the ground, gasping for breath. She felt across her body for blood but found nothing wrong.

Still she cried. Her entire body shook with the spasms of her sobbing.

Then Billy was next to her, rubbing her shoulders. "Sally, what's wrong?"

"I thought I blew up. But Kitty must have saved us."

Sally caught her breath and looked around. It was dark out. Had she been knocked out?

"What are you talking about?" Billy asked.

Sally sat up. They were in the meadow where they had been left by their parents. "How did we get here?"

"We hiked here this morning," Billy said. "We've been waiting for Mom or Dad to come back."

"That's not possible. First there was the catapult, and then we chased the dogs, and then we fought Big Baby."

Billy shook his head. "Nope. Just us here shivering and starving in the meadow. And that thing in the woods watching us."

"Wait, what?" Sally followed his gaze to the edge of the meadow where a pair of eyes glowed.

"It's been watching us all night, ever since the sun went down."

Sally looked again. Something about the glowing eyes seemed familiar. "Kitty?"

A cat meowed and emerged from the shadows.

"Here Kitty."

The cat crept closer in the dark and then walked right up to Sally.

"How do you know this cat?" Billy asked.

"She was in my dream."

"I hope that's all that crawls out of the woods because you were having some terrible dreams."

Sally opened her arms and Kitty crawled into her lap and purred.

"I don't know much about cats," Billy said, "but I'm sure we're not supposed to pet strays in the woods."

"It's fine. She loves us."

Billy stroked the cat, and they passed the rest of the night huddled together.

Mom and Dad arrived after dawn the next morning.

They were super apologetic, as adults are when they do dumb things to kids, especially their own. And Sally and Billy were so relieved to have survived the night and to see their parents again that they all wept tears of joy.

"But we can't keep this cat," Mom said. "We aren't cat people."

"We are now," Sally said.

"Yeah," Billy said. "We have to keep it."

"But it's not our thing to own," Sally said. "Kitty can make up her own mind. I hope she wants to live with us."

Even though Sally had been dreaming, she thought differently of Billy because he had cared about Kitty so strongly that he convinced Sally to do the right thing and help save her.

Sally also thought fondly of Wendy, who had risked her life and suffered great abuse just for the chance she might help Sally, as someone she hoped to meet someday.

And Sally cried when she thought of Tommy, who had been someone that cared about nothing but changed his mind about that and gave his life trying to help Sally and Billy.

Sally was delighted that Kitty decided to live with them. In quiet moments, when there were no adults around, Kitty and Sally talked. Together they worried about the man Billy might become, and wondered what sort of woman Sally wanted to be.

And they became the best of friends. Friends who would do anything for each other.

Sally realized that was what the world needed most, for people to help each other get through their day. One day at a time, day after day.

And she knew in her heart she would become that kind of woman when she was older, and she would have Billy, Wendy, Tommy, and Kitty to thank for it.

Mickey Hadick

Acknowledgments

Thanks to Erin Bartels for editing this story. She gave me a crash course in proper storytelling.

Thanks to Michael Reibsome whose artwork graces these pages, and tells a better story with pictures than I do with words.

Thanks to my early readers, Bob Lapinski, Michael Reid, Elizabeth Colburn, Anita Fox and Shannon Hilliard.

Great thanks to Brian Wallace, poet, friend and shipmate. He has read all I've written, and found a way to correct without discouraging.

Thanks, as always, to my family for putting up with me.

The epigraph is lifted from Life of Brian by Monty Python.

And a special shout-out to Falwell V. Flynt and Kevin M. Smith. Thanks for having my back.

About the Author

Mickey Hadick lives near Lansing, Michigan where he has worked on short stories, novels, screenplays, and books for the past couple of decades.

He was born in Cleveland but ended up in Michigan by way of Pennsylvania.

Whenever possible, he's telling stories, telling jokes, or messing around with computers.

He lives with his wife, two children, and a cat or two.

If you enjoyed these stories and would like to get in on deals for future books, join him at www.mickeyhadick.com.

Made in the USA
Columbia, SC
11 February 2018